PHILIPPA

THE LADY AT THE INN

Complete and Unabridged

LINFORD
Leicester

First published in Great Britain in 2021

First Linford Edition
published 2022

*A catalogue record for this book is available
from the British Library.*

ISBN 978–1–4448–4825–0

Published by
Ulverscroft Limited
Anstey, Leicestershire

Printed and bound in Great Britain by
TJ Books Ltd., Padstow, Cornwall

This book is printed on acid-free paper

THE LADY AT THE INN

Amanda is nineteen years old, very beautiful, very wealthy, orphaned and half-Bengali. She moves from Calcutta to London, to live with her uncle, but he is prejudiced against her Indian appearance and her Indian servants, so when she is abandoned at a country inn by a fortune hunter, he disowns her. The innkeeper doesn't know what to do with his distressed foreign lady guest, so he appeals for help from his landlord, the Earl of Twyford . . .

Maidenhead, Berkshire, 1819

'My lord!' the landlord of the Rose and Crown Inn called. 'Thank goodness you are here, I have urgent need of your advice and assistance.'

Edmund, the Earl of Twyford, had spent most of the day riding around his tenant farms. Now he was hot, tired and in need of a cold drink before going home. He was only a mile from Twyford Hall, but many years ago he had developed the custom of calling now and again at the inn for a mug of ale.

It was, after all, his inn, being part of the Twyford Estate, and he liked to see it was being run properly. He imagined he was considered a trifle eccentric, by drinking in the public bar with the common people, but it was a good way of finding out what was going on in the locality.

The regulars were used to it by now and didn't hesitate to chat with him, even if he was the earl and the landlord

1

for many of them.

'Certainly, Mr Thomas, but I'm parched, so draw me a mug of your best bitter while you tell me all about it.'

'Well, sir, a lady and gentleman arrived earlier from London in a travelling coach. The lady and her maid came into the parlour for some lunch while the gennelman spoke to the postillion.

'Foreign-looking, both the lady and her maid. Her manservant what attends them is foreign and pretty fierce-looking, too. Gave everybody the shivers, he did.

'Anyhow, the ostlers said to me later how it turned out to be a hired vehicle and the postillion wouldn't go no further without extra money.

'By all accounts he'd been paid for a round trip only to Maidenhead and not almost as far as Henley. He wouldn't budge without being paid the extra, so the gentleman went up to join the lady for lunch.

'Before very long I heard them have a huge row and he came storming back downstairs and out to the yard. Then he

2

went off in the coach back towards London and left the lady behind with her servants.

'They've taken rooms and I don't know what's going on nor how long they're going to stay. She says at least tonight, maybe longer, depending when her uncle comes to collect her.

'The lady obviously wasn't planning to stay and so her maid asked if we have any reading books to pass the time. We hadn't, because nobody comes here to read books, do they?

'Now, like I said, the lady and her servants are all foreign-looking, and her manservant in particular is a fierce creature and won't let me speak to the lady; it has to be my wife who goes up there. I don't know where they're from.

'The lady told the wife how she had been deceived by the gentleman, who weren't her husband nor any kind of relation. I wonder, sir, if you could speak to the lady and see what you make of it all?'

Edmund put his hand up to stop the

long flow of words while he drank his beer and absorbed what he had been told.

'Are you saying, then, the lady has been abandoned here?'

'Yes, looks like it, sir, with her servants and only a very small bit of baggage, too.'

'I see. She hasn't asked to hire another vehicle?'

'No, sir. She wrote a letter what we sent down to the Bell to catch the mail coach when it called. My wife didn't think she looked the sort of lady as would want to travel back to London on the stage or the mail.'

'Is she a refined lady, then?'

The landlord nodded.

'She is, sir; speaks nicely and well dressed too. Probably used to travelling privately, not on the stage or the mail. Mind you, I don't know if she's respectable, if you know what I mean. After all, she came with a man who she says were no relation to her.'

Edmund pondered.

'Did you see who the letter was addressed to?'

The landlord shook his head.

'No, sir. My reading's not good and besides, it were a rush to catch the mail. She told the wife it were to her uncle in London so's he would come and get her.'

'So, as she hasn't tried to leave, do you think she can't afford transport or might not be able to pay for her board and lodging?'

'I don't know, my lord.' The man looked concerned. 'I'm worried it might be so, seeing as she didn't ask about hiring a carriage — not that we have one for hire anyway.

'No, she hadn't tried to leave, but just wrote the letter. I'm sure it's all well and good iffen her uncle comes to get her. Don't see many foreigners around here, do we? So don't know who her uncle might be.

'Anyways, it's a funny business and I would be grateful for your opinion, sir. After all, neither you nor I want the Rose and Crown to get a reputation for strange goings-on.'

Edmund finished the last of his beer

and put the mug on the counter.

'If you will ask your good wife to show me up there, I'll see what I can find out.'

Edmund followed the landlady upstairs to where she knocked on a door. The door opened suddenly and she stepped back in fright.

The open doorway revealed a dark-skinned man with a large black moustache and narrowed eyes, a colourful, close-fitting woven cap on his head. He was a little shorter than Edmund, but looked very muscular and had a fierce scowl on his face. There was a large dagger of some sort in his belt.

He looked at the landlady, then at Edmund and his frown deepened. Edmund could see why the landlord described the manservant as fierce.

'I am the Earl of Twyford and would like to speak to your mistress if she can spare me a moment.'

'No.'

'No?' Edward blinked at the terse reply. The man just stood there, not moving, with his arms crossed and scowling at Edmund, who wondered what to do. The man was clearly not going to let him pass or speak with the lady.

Edmund had no reason or desire to force his way in, so there was little help he could offer and little he could tell Mr Thomas, if they didn't even want to talk to him.

'Please tell your mistress she may send me a message if she is in need of assistance, I live nearby.'

Edmund offered his card, but the man didn't move to take it and just stood there immovable and glaring at Edmund. There didn't seem to be anything else to do, so Edmund turned and went back downstairs. He heard the door close behind him.

Back down in the bar he shook his head at the landlord.

'I'm sorry, her manservant wouldn't let me speak to her. If you take a tray up later, put my card on it.' He put his card on the bar, carefully choosing a dry spot. 'You know where I am if you need me. Let me know what happens, won't you?'

'Aye, I'll do so, my lord. Thank you for trying.'

Edmund went out to collect his horse, thinking about the strange circumstances, the fierce manservant and whom his mistress might be. Certainly they were not typical customers of the Rose and Crown.

If they were from India, which was his guess, what on earth were they doing in Maidenhead? And why were they being taken to Henley by a gentleman who apparently couldn't afford the cost of a coach and pair?

It was a peculiar business with more questions than answers.

His curiosity stirred, Edmund decided that instead of waiting for information from the landlord, he might just call again tomorrow to see what had happened in the meantime.

As he wheeled his horse, he caught a glimpse of a pretty face at an upper window; a face which quickly withdrew from sight. A face with brown skin, dark hair and black eyes.

As he trotted home, Edmund mused more about this curious business. It seemed the lady was young and pretty, unless of course, the face at the window had been her maid.

He recalled she had asked for a book to read. This might be a way to satisfy his curiosity. When he got home he would ask his sister for a couple of books to lend to the mystery lady and then send a footman with them to the Rose and Crown.

Tomorrow morning, before the lady's uncle had time to collect her, he would take Geraldine to meet her. Then, after the offer to lend her some books, surely the lady would be polite enough to admit his sister? Geraldine could find out for him the identity of this mysterious lady with the exotic servants.

Six Months Previously, in Calcutta

It was a convenient fiction, Amanda thought. The household would run perfectly well without any guidance from her for quite a long time. All the servants knew this was the case, but they pretended they didn't.

However, if she wasn't called upon to talk to people and make decisions, Amanda knew she would just curl up in a corner and weep. The servants seemed to understand this as well, because since her mother had died some three weeks before, they had referred to her for anything and everything. It appeared their sympathy took the form of keeping her busy while she got over her distress.

Now, just as she was coming to terms with the loss of her mother, her father had fallen ill, too. It was quite clear he was suffering from the same disease that had taken her mother.

The physician had done little for her father, except to prescribe plenty of tea for when he was awake. However, his bouts of fever and unconsciousness were getting longer and longer.

The doctor had said optimistic words to her, but he didn't sound sincere and she didn't believe him for a moment. Amanda was quite sure her father was actually dying from the illness which had taken her mother before.

She bit her lip and held back tears, as she thought about the imminent prospect losing her father as well.

She was roused from her musings by the voice of Debjani, her maid.

'Misa Amanda, come, the master is awake and asking for you.'

She hurried to her father's room. He looked tired, but his eyes sought her as she entered the room.

'Father, shall I give you more tea?'

'No, my child, come and sit by me,' he said in a weak, trembling voice, 'there are things I must tell you before I am gone and I do not think I will last much longer.'

'Father, no! Don't say that.' Amanda lifted her father's hand to her wet cheek as she sat on the edge of his bed.

'I'm sorry, Amanda, but I am afraid I will be joining your mother soon. It's not long since my dear Chandra was taken from me and we all know I have the same sickness.

'Now you must listen carefully, I may not have much more time. When the fever takes me once more, as it surely will, I fear I may not be able to speak to you ever again.

On the table here is my will.' He waved feebly towards the bedside table.

'Everything is left to you, but you may need to prove it. When I am gone, you must go to your uncle Henry in London. It's time you found a husband and London is the best place to find a man whom you can love.

'However, I have appointed your great aunt Janet as your guardian, because I do not trust my brother Henry. He is the whole reason I was sent to Calcutta in the first place, but unfortunately he is also the only one in London who can help you.'

'Why, what did . . .'

His hand fluttered dismissively before it fell back to the bed sheet.

'Never mind now, it is in the past and I have been happy here in Bengal. I don't regret coming here. Aunt Janet is old now and lives in Edinburgh, but I don't want you in Henry's control.

'There is also a letter to my bankers in London. You will be a wealthy woman, but do not tell anyone. Henry was always greedy and will surely try to get his hands on your money, and if it's not him, then it will be fortune hunters. You should conceal from everybody how much money you really have.

'You are nineteen and it is past time you were thinking of marriage, but promise me you will only marry for love, as your mother and I did. Be on your guard. Take your maid Debjani with you and Ramesh as your manservant. You can trust them both. Ramesh has sworn an oath to me to protect you from harm.

Go nowhere without him.'

Amanda's father started to cough and when he paused, she held a glass of water to his lips.

'You're a good girl, Amanda, but I am tired and must rest now.'

Later that day, his fever returned and he never awoke from it. Amanda was desolate and only kept from dissolving into a heap by the need to do so many things.

She and Debjani packed a selection of their clothes into strong trunks for the journey to London. The remainder they gave to the female servants. She and Ramesh selected items of monetary or sentimental value which they packed into more trunks. Other things they gave to the male servants.

In addition, all the servants were given parting gifts of money. The house she gave to her Bengali uncle and her horse to her Bengali cousins. There were many neighbours and also various people from her father's office who called to offer condolences.

One colleague of her father even offered her marriage, which she kindly declined. It would only have been a marriage of convenience for both of them and she remembered her father's words.

★ ★ ★

Finally they boarded a ship for London via the Cape of Good Hope.

Amanda was nervous and filled with doubts about going to a new land where she knew nobody and life must surely be strange.

She had wondered if it would be better to go to her mother's family, but knew in her heart it wouldn't work. They were a merchant family whose business she understood, but her Bengali uncle would never fully accept a niece like Amanda. She had independent ideas, strong opinions and would find it difficult to be obedient to a man.

On the other hand, her father's family were minor aristocrats in England. She wasn't sure she would fit into society any better over there, but it was what her father thought she should do, even if he was estranged from them.

Amanda didn't really know if her English uncle would be any more accepting than her Bengali uncle, so she simply had to trust her father and do what he wanted of her.

She stood on deck, with Debjani and Ramesh either side of her, as they looked out over Calcutta. Soon the tide would come up the river and the ship would start sailing down the River Hoogly to the Bay of Bengal and then a four or five months' voyage to London.

Amanda was glad to hear the wind was favourable for the 100-mile journey down river to the sea. It meant their departure was unlikely to be delayed and they should be in the open ocean well before it became hot and humid in Calcutta.

'Debjani, are you entirely sure you want to come with me to England? If you want to stay here with your family I shall understand.'

'No, Misa Amanda, I have been with

you and your mother since you were a little baby. I cannot leave you now.'

'And you, Ramesh, are you sure you would not prefer to stay here?'

'No, Misa Amanda, I have sworn to your father I will go wherever you go and I am happy to follow you. Wherever I am, I will always have the Himalayas in my heart, so let us go to England.'

Fear of the Unknown

Four months later, they arrived in London on an early morning high tide and with the rising sun behind them. As they slowly came up the river, Amanda could see a forest of ships' masts, far more than she had seen in Calcutta or Cape Town. Further west, there was a smoky haze over the city.

Amanda was glad their journey was coming to an end, although she felt a certain amount of trepidation about her next steps. The novelty of the sea voyage had quickly turned to tedium, only relieved now and again by storms or sightings of whales and other ships.

It was reassuring to have Debjani and Ramesh with her on arrival in London and thus not be totally alone in a city full of strangers.

By late morning they were arriving at her uncle Baron Walsh's house in Wimpole Street. At the docks, Ramesh had hired a cart for their baggage and then a hackney carriage for the ladies.

He was a cautious man and travelled with the baggage to make sure it all followed the hackney and didn't suddenly disappear off into the city, never to be seen again. As they drew up in Wimpole Street, he sprang down from the baggage cart and applied the door knocker vigorously, while Debjani assisted Amanda from the hackney. The door opened and a footman appeared, only to take a quick step back at the sight of Ramesh standing in the doorway.

As Amanda stepped down to the pavement, she looked around. She had seen a variety of houses on their way from the docks and hadn't been quite sure what to expect.

This street was full of relatively recent and substantial terraced houses, but she thought them rather plain and uninspiring. Therefore, she concluded, a certain amount of money, but perhaps not a great deal of it.

Father had said, some time ago, her grandfather had been comfortable without being wealthy and Uncle Henry would have inherited it all. It did not appear he had expanded his fortune.

'Miss Buckley has arrived,' Ramesh said to the footman. 'Come, there is baggage to be unloaded.'

A butler appeared beside the footman and waved him to follow Ramesh, who had not waited for the footman before turning back to the cart.

'Good morning, Miss Buckley,' the butler said, 'you have been expected, but the family have yet to rise. I am Mr Keith and this is Mrs Donnelly, the housekeeper, who will show you to your room. I will advise his lordship of your arrival in due course.'

'Mr Keith, Mrs Donnelly,' Amanda said, acknowledging them both with a slight nod. 'This is my maid Debjani. The man supervising the baggage is my manservant Ramesh whom you may not have been expecting, but who will also require a room.'

Their eyebrows twitched, but there was no questioning Amanda's commanding tone.

'Yes, miss, I will attend to it shortly,' Mrs Donnelly said. 'If you would follow me please?'

Amanda and Debjani followed her upstairs, Debjani clutching a jewel case to her chest. They went up two floors and then down a corridor to the room at the end.

'This is your room, Miss Buckley. Miss Letitia and Miss Felicity have the rooms opposite. I will have a truckle bed installed in the adjoining dressing-room for your maid. Your manservant will have a room upstairs with the footmen.'

Amanda and Debjani went in as the housekeeper went off to arrange a bed for Ramesh.

'I don't know where we will put everything,' Debjani said, looking around the bed chamber, 'there's not enough room.'

'Yes, I had expected something a little larger,' Amanda said. 'This must be a guest room. Never mind, I'm sure we'll manage somehow. At least it is bigger than the cabin on the ship.'

'True, misa, but then your trunks were

stowed in the ship's hold, not in your cabin.'

Ramesh and footmen had appeared carrying trunks.

'Ramesh, just tell them to stack the trunks in the corner for now. Debjani, do you know which one contains the gifts?'

'Yes, misa, and Mrs Donnelly said Lady Walsh had two grown daughters, so three rolls of the silk?'

'Yes, and the gold snuff box from the jewel case.'

'Misa Amanda,' Ramesh said, 'shall I retain the keys to the trunks until we know these people better?'

Amanda hesitated. They were all family or servants of the family. Then she recalled her father saying he didn't trust his brother. There was no harm in a little caution, was there?

'Yes, keep the keys for the time being.'

Once the gifts had been taken out, Ramesh tucked the keys into a pouch on his belt and then went to find his own room.

Amanda changed out of her travelling

dress into a pale yellow jamdani muslin day dress, cut in a western style.

'Debjani, do you think it looks right?'

'Yes, misa, everybody dresses differently here and this one is similar. I don't think a sari would be appropriate, it would be too strange for them. Also, this yellow dress makes a pleasing contrast with the brown of your skin.

'Now sit on the stool while I brush your hair. It is important for you to make a good first impression.'

Very soon there was a gentle tap on the door. Debjani opened it to find it was the butler. He stared at Amanda for a brief moment before recollecting himself.

'Miss Buckley, Lord Walsh asks if you would join him and the family in the drawing-room when it is convenient.'

Amanda took a deep breath. She was a little nervous to be meeting these strangers, even if they were family. And now was as convenient as it would ever be.

'If you would lead the way? Debjani, hand me the snuff box and bring the silks, please.'

They followed the butler down a floor to where he opened some double doors. 'Miss Buckley, sir,' he said, before standing to one side.

Amanda entered the room to find a middle-aged couple and a pair of girls of about her own age. The eyes of the parents widened and the mouths of the girls dropped open.

Amanda wondered why they all looked surprised. Had they had expected a much younger girl, or perhaps someone dowdy? Her uncle recovered from his surprise first.

'Welcome, niece, I am your uncle Henry, this is your aunt Viola and your cousins Letitia and Felicity.'

He indicated each one in turn and they bowed to each other.

'Come and sit with us to tell us about yourself,' he said.

'Thank you, Uncle, I have some gifts for you all. This one is for you,' she said, handing him the snuff box.

'Good heavens,' he said, looking at the

24

engraved gold surface, 'this is uncommonly generous of you.'

She noticed him weigh it in his hand and then flip the top open. As he assessed the box, Amanda assessed him. His first thought appeared be of its value, realising at once it was silver gilt, not solid gold. She considered it a nice gift, but did he have a wild and inflated idea of her wealth? Was he supposing she could afford to give him a solid gold snuffbox? She beckoned Debjani to step forward.

'And these rolls of silk are for you aunt, and for my cousins. I shall leave it to you to decide who will have which colour. I am supposing you have a modiste who can fashion them into evening gowns for you.'

Debjani placed the silks on to a low table and looked to Amanda, who nodded and indicated Debjani may go. The other ladies didn't pay any attention to her maid as they crowded around the table to examine the material.

When Amanda had entered the room, Viola had been both surprised and dismayed. Her niece was not at all how she had imagined her. For some reason, she had expected an unremarkable English girl of perhaps fifteen or sixteen years old.

In the event, the girl who had entered the room was exotically beautiful, older, well dressed and very self-composed. Viola could see immediately how her own daughters were going to be cast into the shade by their cousin whenever they all appeared together. What young man would even look at her daughters when her niece was present?

She was going to have to do some rapid re-planning. Finding husbands for her daughters would be difficult while their cousin was around. She glanced at her girls to make the comparison. From the look on their faces, Letitia and Felicity thought much the same as their mother.

Viola considered what could be done. Amanda looked foreign, but if she was as rich as they expected, it should not be difficult to find someone to take her off their hands. There must be men prepared to overlook her brown skin and dark eyes in exchange for a large injection of money.

After all, there were peers without money who were happy to give their titles in exchange for a rich American bride, weren't there? However, while American brides looked much the same as English brides, this certainly wasn't the case here. Amanda had distinctly Indian features, but except for those, it was more or less the same exchange, wasn't it? Yes, definitely, the quicker her niece was married off, the better.

Then Amanda gave Viola's husband a gold snuff box. Gold! And her maid had put rolls of silk on the coffee table. Not just dress lengths, but rolls. Probably enough for dozens of dresses each. The sooner they could get Amanda out in society and she could spread the word of her niece being wealthy, the better.

In the meantime, she needed to find out a little more and tea would be just the thing. She supposed that, coming from India, Amanda would prefer tea to coffee.

'Letitia, kindly ring for the tea tray. Felicity, move the silks to the other sofa if you please,' Viola said, as they sat around the table. 'Tell me, my dear, do you have ball gowns?' Viola asked. If she didn't, getting some made was obviously the first priority.

'Yes, I have several. Perhaps, later on today, you could look at them for me to see if the style is suitable for London? I know news from London gets to Calcutta months later and it could be my gowns are sadly out of date, too.'

Viola looked at Amanda's day dress thoughtfully. The material was very fine and, if she was not mistaken, there were some fine gold threads running through it. When people saw it, they might not care if the gown was the latest style or not. Nobody else would be wearing a gown with gold in the material.

'I'm sure we will manage. Might Letitia and Felicity see them, too? I'm sure they will be interested.'

'Oh, yes, please, cousin,' Letitia said, 'we would love to see what you have brought with you.'

'And Mama,' Felicity said, 'you must give our cousin some lotion for her skin. She has become sadly brown and tanned during the sea voyage.'

Amanda looked down at her hands and arms, turning them to look at her skin. They looked perfectly normal to her. Thus it was she didn't notice her aunt frowning at Felicity and shaking her head a little, while Letitia jabbed an elbow into her sister's ribs.

Then, as Amanda thought about her cousin's remark, she saw how Felicity could not have seen many people from hot countries. By contrast, her aunt and cousins had very pale complexions, so Felicity's mistake was easy to understand.

In the afternoon, the ladies all trooped up to Amanda's room to inspect her wardrobe.

'Cousin Amanda,' Felicity said, 'why do you have so many trunks in your room?'

'Because we have left Calcutta for good, we needed to bring all our clothes and many items from my house. The items have little value; they are mostly sentimental. Pictures of my parents, one or two of my school books, a few favourite ornaments, that sort of thing. Things I would have been sad to leave behind.'

'Which ones have your dresses?' Letitia asked.

'My maid Debjani knows and a footman has gone to find Ramesh, my manservant, because he has all the keys.'

A short while later, Ramesh arrived and Debjani told him which ones to lift down and open. The two sisters stood there staring in amazement at the fierce-looking Ramesh and how he seemed to be moving the trunks effortlessly.

'Amanda,' Felicity whispered, 'is that a sword your manservant is wearing in the house?'

'Ah, that is a kukri, the traditional weapon of a Gurkha,' Amanda said, 'come closer while I tell you about it.' The girls leaned in conspiratorially. 'They say,' Amanda whispered, 'if it is removed from the sheath it must draw blood before it is replaced.' The girls draw a sharp breath and their eyes widened.

'And also,' Amanda continued quietly, 'if it is thrown at an enemy it will take his head clean off.'

The girls squeaked with fright as Ramesh turned at looked them with narrowed eyes, lowered brows and a toothy grin.

'But it's not really true, it's just a story,' Amanda said in a normal voice. 'I've seen him use it to cut fruit, but it's a good one, isn't it?'

Ramesh left the room, chuckling quietly to himself, while the two sisters giggled nervously.

In the evening they all sat down to dinner for the first time together.

'Amanda,' her aunt said, 'I saw you have brought a manservant with you, as well as your maid. When he goes back to India, will you be sending your maid home with him as well?'

'Sending them home? Oh, no, they will not be going back to India, they will both stay here with me.'

'But don't you wish to employ an English lady's maid now you are here?'

'Oh, no, absolutely not, I wouldn't dream of it. Debjani has been with me since I was a little girl and I could never send her away. Before we left, I asked her if she wanted to remain in India and she quite emphatically said she wanted to come with me. No, I could never replace her.'

'Well, what about this manservant of yours?' the baron asked. 'Surely he is going back?'

Amanda was a little irritated. Didn't she just say they were both staying? Was her uncle not hearing anything he didn't want to hear?

'No, he's not going back, either. He was also given the choice, but he insisted on coming with me.'

'He insisted?'

'Oh, yes. He swore a solemn oath to my father to stay with me and protect me.'

'Well, I don't like the idea of heathens in my house, wearing weapons and corrupting the morals of the other servants.'

'Heathens? They're not heathens! They're both Christians, like you or me. I admit Ramesh was a Hindu in his youth, as most people are in Nepal, but he converted to Anglicanism a long time ago. I assume you are Anglicans, not Roman Catholic or Jewish?'

'Of course we're Anglicans!' her uncle said, getting red in the face and thumping the table.

'Now then, dear,' her aunt said, 'Amanda didn't mean any offence. I'm sure there are lots of different religions in India, just as we have more than one here.'

'Yes, but we have proper religions here and I still don't like the idea. He'll be frightening the maids. I think you should tell him to go home,' her uncle said.

Amanda was quickly forming a dislike of her uncle. He seemed to have rigid opinions and not be at all open to new ideas. She would have to try hard to be civil and not aggravate him. She was, after all, a guest in his house.

'I'm sorry, Uncle, but it would be

a waste of my breath to tell him to go back to India. He's a very loyal man and wouldn't dream of breaking his word to my father. As to him corrupting the other servants, it's quite impossible, he is an entirely honourable man.'

'Cousin Amanda,' Letitia said, 'what did you mean, he is from Nepal? Is he not Indian?'

Amanda was grateful for the slight change of direction.

'No, Nepal is in the Himalayan mountains north of India. He is a kind of Nepali warrior called a Gurkha. They have a fearsome reputation as brave and courageous fighters, which is why my father knew I would be safe if he travelled with me.'

'Oh, I see now why he wears his strange knife all the time,' Letitia said.

'He wears a strange knife?'

'Oh, yes, Father, he . . . '

'Letitia!' Amanda interrupted. 'Please remember the story I told you is only a legend, and I doubt your father will want to hear any such details at the dinner table.'

Amanda really didn't want everything getting out of hand and thus providing her uncle with more reasons for Ramesh to leave.

'He always wears a ceremonial knife which can also be used as a weapon if necessary. It is why my father knew he would make a good bodyguard.'

'I don't know what the world is coming to when a footman wears a weapon,' her uncle said. 'What will people say?'

'I'm sure, Uncle, they will think it is very progressive of you to provide armed protection for the ladies of your family. It might even start a new fashion.'

He didn't look convinced or happy, but he did turn his attention back to the food, for which Amanda was grateful.

'Now we have seen Amanda's ball gowns, I have sent acceptances for the Morton's ball tomorrow evening,' Aunt Viola said.

Amanda thought the other ladies all looked pleased at the prospect. Her uncle simply grunted.

A Wise Move

'Keith, would you call a hackney for us, please?' Amanda asked the butler.

Mr Keith looked surprised to see them not only out of bed, but dressed and going out at only nine o'clock in the morning. He recovered his poise and surveyed the three of them about to depart.

'Begging your pardon, miss, but a hackney only has room for two persons. Will you be requiring two hackneys?'

Amanda realised this was something she hadn't even noticed or thought about on their way from the docks.

'Oh. I see. No, there is no need. Debjani, you may stay here and Ramesh will come with me.'

Keith sent a footman outside to find a cab.

'May I tell her ladyship where you have gone, miss, and when to expect you back?'

'I have business in the city which should not take very long and I expect to be back quite soon. Is it very far to Fleet Street?'

'Perhaps fifteen minutes in the hackney, miss.'

Less than twenty minutes later, Amanda was entering a bank in Fleet Street, followed by Ramesh. A clerk approached her, cautiously eyeing Ramesh, who in turn was watching him over Amanda's shoulder.

'Good morning, ma'am, may I help you?'

'Yes, I would like to see the manager. You may tell him Miss Buckley, newly arrived from India, wishes to speak with him.'

'Very good, miss, I will see if he is available,' the clerk said, before he scuttled off into the gloom of the bank. He came back very quickly. 'If you would follow me please, Mr Hoare will see you immediately.'

Mr Hoare was standing behind a large desk deep inside the bank. His office was large and expensively furnished.

'Good morning, Miss Buckley, I

received a letter from your father a few months ago warning me to expect you. Please take a seat. Am I to assume the worst?'

As Amanda sat in front of the desk, a clerk hurried in and placed a folder on the desk, before hurrying out again and closing the office door. Ramesh stood a few paces behind her with his arms crossed.

'I am afraid so, Mr Hoare. My father passed away some five months ago and I have moved to London as he wished. I have a letter of introduction from him.'

'My condolences, Miss Buckley. I shall be glad to be of any assistance I can provide.'

She passed a folded paper across the desk. Mr Hoare opened it, skimmed the contents briefly and passed it back.

'Thank you. May I make a note of where you are staying?'

'I am living with my uncle, Baron Walsh, in Wimpole Street.'

He made a quick annotation in the folder.

'From your father's letter, I believe you are his sole beneficiary?'

'Yes. I have his will with me if you wish to see it.'

'Since he had already written to me to this effect, it will not be necessary, thank you. I am sure you realise you are a wealthy lady now, but I believe you are not yet of age?'

'That is correct.'

'And is your uncle your guardian?'

'No, he is not. My guardian is a great aunt who lives in Edinburgh. A Mrs Janet Johnstone of George Square.'

'Edinburgh?' He rubbed his chin thoughtfully. 'I see. This could be inconvenient. But, wait a moment if you please . . . ' He rummaged in the file and extracted a letter, which he read carefully.

'Ah yes, I see your father expressly wished you to have sole control of your fortune. This is a trifle irregular when you are under age, but as you are hardly a child, I'm sure we need not consider the matter further.' He smiled reassuringly at his rich client.

'Let me be very clear on this important point,' she said. 'My uncle is not to have authority of any kind whatsoever over my account, and furthermore, I do not wish anyone, especially not my uncle, to be aware of how much I may have in my account.'

'I understand, Miss Buckley, and you may rest assured that all of your dealings with the bank will remain strictly confidential.'

'Very good. Mr Hoare, it is my intention at present to draw a small quarterly sum and it is likely my manservant Ramesh here,' she pointed behind her, 'will bring a request on my behalf each time and collect it for me. He may also call with a draft for different amounts on various other occasions. Initially, I anticipate perhaps two hundred pounds per quarter will suffice. Is this arrangement convenient?'

'Quite convenient. Do you wish such a sum this morning?'

'If you would, please.'

He rang a bell on his desk. A clerk

came in, listened to some quiet instructions, and hurried out again.

'Would you care for tea, Miss Buckley?'

'Thank you, no. I'm sure you are a busy man and I mean to return home before the household is fully awake.'

'Quite so,' he said, nodding an understanding. 'Ah, here is your money.'

The returning clerk placed some banknotes, a small bag of coins and a slip of paper on the desk. The bank manager handed her a quill.

'If you would be good enough to sign the receipt which I will also retain in the file as evidence of your signature.'

Amanda signed the receipt, then stood and handed the money to Ramesh. He tucked it into the pouch on his belt. She shook Mr Hoare's hand.

'It has been a pleasure to meet you, Miss Buckley and I hope to be of service in the future.' He opened the office door and escorted her to the front door of the bank, where he sent a junior out to hail a hackney cab.

★ ★ ★

A little later that morning, Amanda was in the morning-room reading a newspaper to understand current events in London and England.

'Excuse me, Miss Buckley,' a footman said, 'the baron asks you to attend him in his study as soon as convenient.'

Amanda folded the newspaper and stood.

'Would you show me the way, please?'

The footman showed her the way to the study and tapped on the door before opening it.

'Miss Buckley, sir.'

'You wanted to speak to me, Uncle?'

'Yes, Amanda, I thought we should call on your bankers without delay.'

Well, Amanda thought, her father was right and Uncle Henry was wasting no time. No doubt he hoped to get control of her money without delay.

'There is no need, Uncle, I already called on them first thing this morning and everything is in order.'

'You called on them? But how is this? You are under age and as your guardian I will need to go with you so they will know to accept my instructions.'

Amanda reflected it had been smart of her to go to the bank without delay. It might have been awkward and confusing if her uncle had demanded to take control.

Even though the bank had clear instructions from her father giving Amanda control of her money, they might have been inclined to listen to a man first, especially if he was claiming to be her guardian. As it was, both she and the bank were clear on how things stood.

'Oh, but Uncle, you are not my guardian. My guardian is Great-aunt Janet.'

'What? Aunt Janet? No, this cannot be, it is absurd. She is very old, lives in Edinburgh and is quite unsuitable. She is undoubtedly infirm and I don't think she was entirely of sound mind the last time I saw her. Are quite you sure you haven't misunderstood?'

'Oh, yes,' Amanda said, as innocently

as she could, 'Father told me so and it was specified in his will, too. Perhaps at the time he wrote it, he was thinking I would go to Edinburgh instead of London.'

Her uncle frowned and shook his head.

'Oh, no, no. This will not do. How can she administer your fortune from Edinburgh? And besides, she probably has no idea what should be done. I will write to her and ask her to relinquish her guardianship to me, it's the only way which makes sense.'

Amanda made a mental note to write to her great-aunt as well and beg her to do no such thing.

'But Uncle, wouldn't it be a lot of trouble for a trifling amount of money?' Of course, she thought, one person's trifle could be another fortune, could it not? She didn't want to lie outright, but one could be a little vague, couldn't one? And if people made assumptions, then surely it was their problem, not hers?

'Trifling? But surely your father was

wealthy and he left it all to you?'

She thought a delicate amount of evasion might be tactful. She didn't want to antagonise her uncle if she was to live here, did she?

'The bank manager thought if I was prudent, the capital should last me several years. Naturally, I hope to marry before long, so then it may become my dowry. In the circumstances, the manager saw no need to involve a guardian.

'I arranged with him I would draw a small amount each quarter. I shall need to pay my servants and then I thought to give you half of the drawn amount as my contribution towards the household expenses.'

'I think this would be appropriate, yes, but how much will it be?' her uncle said, looking puzzled at the unexpected turn of events.

'If I give you one hundred pounds each quarter, then I shall keep whatever is left as pin money after I have paid my servants.'

Her uncle deflated. He was clearly

very shocked and disappointed, even though Amanda was very sure the extra cost of her living here would be considerably less than one hundred pounds a quarter.

Her father hadn't trusted his brother and she fully suspected her uncle had been expecting to add a very large amount of money to his own. It wasn't going to happen. Amanda was glad to be one step ahead of her uncle.

She was grateful to be given a home in London, but after his hurtful remarks about her servants, she wasn't sure how welcome she, or they, really were. If his welcome was purely mercenary, it might be temporary, too, if he saw her as troublesome or inconvenient.

Amanda could see a time might come, and perhaps before very long, when she would need to establish her own household elsewhere. Before she did so, she needed to make some acquaintances in society if she was not then to become isolated.

If her own relations objected to her

background, who knew what other people might also say about the appearance of herself and her servants? She needed to meet other people before deciding to strike out on her own.

Amanda saw her idea of volunteering a contribution to the household had probably been a good one. She had judged the amount was enough to be appreciated, but small enough not to give rise to speculation. However, it appeared the appreciation was as small as the expectation had been large.

Night of the Ball

'Viola, we need to talk about Amanda,' the baron said.

'Yes, we do. She is pretty in her own way, but I never expected her to be so brown. Even so, she will distract the young men from our daughters with her exotic looks. Then, when the novelty has worn off, it will be recalled we have Indian blood in the family and it will be difficult for our own daughters to make advantageous marriages.

'It's fortunate Amanda is a rich heiress so we can get her married off quickly. She can take those barbaric servants with her, too, when she goes as well.'

'But that's just it. She isn't a rich heiress,' the baron said, shaking his head sorrowfully.

His wife looked at him in surprise.

'She isn't? But you said your brother was prosperous and doing well.'

'I think my brother must have been exaggerating, just in order to spite me.

Far from being a senior manager in the East India Company, I now wonder if he was just a clerk in one of their counting houses.'

His wife shook her head.

'No, I don't believe it. Have you seen the quality of the silks in her wardrobe?'

'Perhaps silk and seamstresses are much cheaper in India. From what I've heard before, the servants cost little and the silk must undoubtedly be cheaper there, too.

'No, from what I can work out, she has no more than a few thousand to her name. Far from being an asset to the family, she is a liability.'

'What on earth are we to do? Obviously we need somebody to take her off our hands as soon as possible, but how?'

The baron tapped his nose conspiratorially.

'I think at the ball this evening we let it be known she has a fortune of her own. We don't need to say how much and if someone asks, we shall simply say we don't know.'

Viola mulled it over for a couple of minutes.

'Yes, but when some man asks you for her hand and wants to talk about settlements, what will you say?'

'I shall refer them to her guardian, who is apparently Aunt Janet up in Edinburgh.'

'Aunt Janet, not you?'

'Yes. I was annoyed at first, but on reflection, it's rather convenient, isn't it? They can write to the old biddy or post up to Scotland, I don't care, but I doubt if she will know anything, nor care much, either.

'After all, she won't know Amanda from Adam, or I should say Eve, will she? She'll probably think the guardianship is just a nuisance. She'll probably approve of anything which is suggested and wash her hands of our niece at the same time.'

Viola smiled as she nodded approval of the plan.

'This means we have no need to provide a dowry either, because she can provide it herself from whatever she has.

I suppose we could host a very modest wedding breakfast when she marries, but then wash our hands of her as well.'

'Exactly. And by the time she is married and her husband discovers how little she has, it will be too late.'

'I shall tell Felicity and Letitia not to tell anyone about Amanda having a fortune and it's to be a secret. They will then undoubtedly tell their friends all about it in confidence.'

* * *

Amanda was excited to be going to her first ball in London. She had been to balls in Calcutta, but this would surely be different. For a start, she expected more aristocratic people and fewer military or merchants. Considering her uncle's attitude yesterday, she hoped she wouldn't be snubbed. Even in Calcutta, there were a few English people who would turn their nose up at her because she was part Indian, even though she was obviously not a servant.

51

As she waited for the others to climb into the carriage, she was happy to see Ramesh standing on the back of it. She suspected the others hadn't noticed him, as nobody had said anything. It was getting dark and servants were often invisible, even in the daytime.

★ ★ ★

Amanda stood behind her cousins on the stairs at the Mortons' house while everybody inched upwards to the receiving line. She couldn't help but notice glances in her direction and some whispering, but she ignored them and held her head high. Finally she arrived in front of her hosts for the evening.

'. . . and this is my niece, Miss Buckley,' the baron said, 'recently arrived from India.'

'Ah, yes, I understand now,' Lady Morton said. 'Don't worry, Miss Buckley, the colour will soon fade.'

Amanda was starting to get irritated and would have liked to give her hostess a sharp set down, but instead, she gritted her teeth, smiled and curtseyed, before following her cousins into the ballroom.

'Letitia, Felicity,' Aunt Viola said, 'Amanda doesn't know anybody, so be so good as take her with you and introduce her to some of your friends and acquaintances.'

Amanda noticed her aunt and uncle give each other a little nod and smile. She was glad she was going to meet some people of her own age. It would have been embarrassing to be a wallflower while she watched her cousins dance. Of course, she was assuming somebody would actually ask her to dance.

'Come along, cousin,' Letitia said, taking her by the arm and heading around the room to a small group of young people talking together.

'Now then, everybody,' she said, 'I wish to introduce my cousin Miss Buckley, who is lately arrived from India.'

As Letitia mentioned her friends' names, a couple of girls looked Amanda up and down in an unfriendly and condescending way. After the brief round of introductions, Letitia turned to a young man whom Amanda thought looked slightly uncomfortable.

'Now then, Freddy, you must not be shy and but instead ask my cousin to dance, I'm sure she would love to.'

She turned to Amanda.

'Freddy Seaton is my best friend's younger brother and quite a good dancer, but he is horribly shy and so we have to push him now and again.'

Freddy swallowed and went bright red.

'Er, um, of course, Miss . . . er, Miss Buckley. Would you, um, care to dance?' he said, and after a moment's hesitation, offered his arm.

Amanda did not care for the way he had been humiliated by Letitia's careless words. It was unkind and uncalled for. And somebody, she wasn't sure whom, had tittered at the exchange.

Amanda felt a great deal of sympathy for him. She of all people knew what it was like to have people make remarks about you as if you weren't standing there. She had had experience of English people condescending to her before in Calcutta, because she had an obviously mixed heritage. It looked as if it might be the same here. Well, she could be kind, even if her cousin and her friends were not.

'Mr Seaton, I would be delighted,' Amanda said, taking his arm and steering him gently towards the dance floor where a set was forming for a country dance.

She had a moment of fear, wondering if it was a dance which she knew. She hadn't heard the name of the dance mentioned. Did they do different dances in London and Calcutta? Well, there was nothing for it now. She would have to watch what everybody else did, and if she didn't recognise it, she would simply have to copy what other ladies were doing as best she could.

'Mr Seaton,' she said quietly, 'I should warn you this is my first dance in London since arriving from Calcutta. I do hope I recognise the steps because I didn't hear the name. If you see me going wrong, please do whisper a hint for the next bit each time we pass. Or, if we remain together, do not hesitate to steer me in the right direction.'

As they took their places she saw he looked rather alarmed and he swallowed nervously. She smiled at him encouragingly and he gave her a slight nod in return. As it happened, she recognised the dance immediately, which was a huge relief.

The dance ended, she took his arm again and guided him towards her aunt, instead of back to Letitia's friends.

'I am most grateful to you, Mr Seaton. This was my first dance at my first ball in London. If it had not been for your kind offer, I might have been a wallflower. Not only this, but I was grateful for your support when I wasn't sure which dance it would be.'

She knew perfectly well she hadn't needed his support, but nevertheless he had been willing to help. After all, when she admitted she had no idea what dance it was going to be, he could have insisted they promenade around the room instead. He might be young and unsure of himself, but he was a gentleman and she liked him.

'I, er, I was very er, happy to dance with you, Miss Buckley, it was my pleasure.'

'My cousin Letitia was quite correct, you are an excellent dancer.'

'Really?'

'Oh, yes, and if you were to ask me again later on, I would be perfectly happy to dance with you once more.'

He swallowed and started to blush again.

'Really?' he squeaked.

'Absolutely. I look forward to next time,' Amanda said. 'Now, here is my aunt, Lady Walsh. Thank you again, Mr Seaton.'

She smiled at him. He was so lacking in confidence, but she thought he had a certain boyish charm and she definitely liked him.

He blinked, bowed, and walked away.

'Amanda, dear,' her aunt said, 'I'm so glad to see you dancing. Here is a gentleman who has been awaiting your return.

Mr Mellor, may I present my niece, Miss Buckley. Amanda, this is Mr Mellor.'

'Mr Mellor,' Amanda said with a curtsey to his bow.

Mr Mellor was slender, had very pleasing regular features and guinea gold curly hair. Some might say he looked a little too pretty and not sufficiently masculine. His dress was impeccable, yet modest and not given to any dandyish features. Altogether he looked like a fashion plate for the man about town. Amanda supposed he used the best tailors in London, not that she had any idea who they might be.

He was surely handsome enough for any of the young ladies here to want to dance with him, so Amanda felt flattered at his attention.

'Miss Buckley, I am hoping you may be free for the next dance,' he said with a captivating and confident smile.

'Indeed I am. I thank you, sir.'

She took the proffered arm and he led her to the dance floor. This time she had paid attention to the name of the dance when it was announced and knew it to be one which was easy and familiar. It was an unexceptional country dance and Mr Mellor proved to be a competent but equally unexceptional dancer, yet with a ready smile.

At the end, he led her back towards Aunt Viola, who was looking pleased with herself.

'Miss Buckley, may I also request the honour of the supper dance, if it is not yet spoken for?'

Amanda's fear of being a wallflower was evaporating quickly.

'Thank you, Mr Mellor, I am free for the supper dance.' She hoped it was not a waltz. She knew of the dance, but had never learned it. She would have to ask her aunt about engaging a dancing master.

As she arrived at her aunt's side, Letitia was already there.

'You lucky thing,' she said, 'only your second dance and the Mellor asks you for it.'

'The Mellor?'

'It's what we call him. He is so good-looking and very particular in whom he asks to dance. I wish he would ask me, but he never has done,' she said with a sniff.

'You are right, he is remarkably handsome, isn't he?'

'Yes, and his father is a viscount and his grandfather is an earl, too. Mind you, he is only a third son and unlikely to inherit, but you never know.'

'Oh, my goodness! I had not realised I was being granted a favour by such an eligible gentleman. He asked me for the supper dance too.'

'What! Oh, this is so unfair,' Letitia said, looking as if she wanted to cry or stamp her foot. 'Cousin, you must tell him to ask me to dance if he wants to retain your good opinion of him.'

Amanda looked at her cousin. If he hadn't asked her cousin before, he probably didn't want to now. She wondered if Letitia wanted to dance with him simply because he made himself exclusive, and dancing with him would be a feather in her cap.

Whatever the case, Amanda didn't mind. Just because her cousin could be unkind to others, there was no need for her to be unkind to Letitia. As it was, she could certainly ask Mr Mellor, rather than tell. Hopefully he wouldn't consider it impertinent.

'Very well, I shall ask him at supper, if he will oblige me by asking you to dance, but naturally I can't force him to do so.'

'Amanda, you are the best of cousins.'

'Am I not your only cousin?' Amanda asked drily.

'Proof enough, then,' Letitia said with a grin.

Mr Mellor was full of questions at supper and Amanda was faintly surprised, as it felt a bit like an interrogation.

He seemed only interested in her background, not of anything else, such the ball itself or her London family. Perhaps he was already familiar with her uncle Henry and family.

She already knew people might have a dim view of her Bengali mother, so was deliberately vague and only spoke in generalities of life in Calcutta.

Perhaps later, when she knew him better, she might tell him more about her family life in Calcutta. When she asked him about himself, he was equally vague and spoke only of his family and their ancestral estate in Buckinghamshire.

'Mr Mellor, may I ask a favour of you?'

He looked suspiciously at her.

'What sort of favour?'

'Nothing of great import. My cousin Letitia would very much like to dance with you. If you were to ask her, we would both be very much obliged to you.'

He frowned, as if he wasn't sure who Letitia was, then then shrugged slightly, as if it didn't matter to him, before smiling.

'Oh, I see. I'm sure I will be happy to do so, since it is you who are asking it of me, Miss Buckley. However, perhaps it would be wise if you took me and introduced me to her after supper. I don't think I have met her and it would not do for me to accidentally mark a dance on the wrong young lady's card, would it?'

'No, indeed, Mr Mellor.'

Which, Amanda thought, was a clever way to avoid saying not only had he probably not met Letitia, but even if he had, he didn't have the faintest idea who Miss Letitia might be. Never mind, Letitia would be happy anyway.

A Pleasing Invitation

'Mr Mellor,' Keith, the butler, announced.

The ladies were in the morning-room ready to receive visits from gentlemen who had danced with the girls on the previous evening. There were already numerous bouquets around the room and a maid hovering in the corner with empty vases in expectation of more.

Mellor stopped in the doorway as he looked around. He was carrying two bouquets, one of yellow roses, the other of red. After a moment's hesitation, Amanda saw him approach Letitia.

He bowed, presented her with the yellow roses and exchanged a few words. Letitia looked extraordinarily pleased and flattered as she bent to smell the flowers. Amanda noticed Felicity, on the far side of Letitia, looked far from pleased. In fact, if looks could kill, her sister would be lying dead on the floor.

Mellor stole a quick glance at Felicity

before bowing again to Letitia and heading to Amanda.

'Miss Buckley, good morning,' he said, offering her the flowers. 'I do hope you care for roses.'

'Thank you, Mr Mellor, they look quite delightful. Please do take a seat. Would you care for tea?' She handed the flowers to the maid for putting into a vase.

'No tea for me, thank you,' he said, sitting beside her. 'I hope you are not too fatigued from the ball?'

'Not at all, Mr Mellor, after several months on board ship it was refreshing to move about and meet new people.'

'I see I have offended a young lady and I must lay the fault at your feet, Miss Buckley.'

'Offended a lady? And it is my fault?'

'Yes, indeed, I was not aware there were two daughters of the baron, and now I have offended one of them by presenting flowers to one and not the other.'

'Ah, yes. But then, you only danced with one of them, did you not?'

'This is true, but it was at your behest. I would have been willing to please you further by dancing with both of them, had I known.'

'Please me?'

'But of course. My dearest wish is your happiness, Miss Buckley,' he said, gazing at her earnestly.

'Mr Mellor! You should not be saying these things; we have barely met.'

'There are times when one knows one's feelings at once, Miss Buckley, and hesitation is useless.'

Amanda thought he was a little too effusive and fulsome for her taste on what was only a second meeting. It was flattering, but a bit too soon for her to feel comfortable. Perhaps flirtatious talk was normal for him, but she wasn't used to it.

'Mr Mellor, there is a simple way for you to make amends and remove the offence.'

'There is?'

'Of course. Before you leave, you could ask Miss Letitia to introduce you to her younger sister, Miss Felicity. You could then ask her to reserve a dance for you at the next ball. At a stroke, you will redeem yourself and restore sisterly harmony.'

Amanda thought this might also be a way to measure his sincerity and see, if instead, he was just a flatterer mouthing empty words. She noticed he sighed slightly before responding.

'Very well, Miss Buckley, I shall do as you ask. However,' he said, raising a finger, 'it is contingent upon you allowing me to drive you in the park tomorrow afternoon.'

She had been hoping for a drive in the park at the fashionable hour with a handsome gentleman. She had heard all about it and was more than happy to accept.

'I shall be delighted, sir, provided, of course, that my aunt approves.'

'Until tomorrow, then,' he said and lifted her fingers to his lips.

Amanda watched as he headed towards Letitia. They exchanged a few words before they both went to Felicity.

Amanda couldn't see or hear what they said, but as he walked away she could see Felicity was sitting there frozen, with her hand half raised, her jaw dropped open, her eyes wide and a silly smile on her face. Well, thought Amanda, it appeared both she, Letitia and Mr Mellor had all done their good deed for the day.

It also occurred to her he hadn't waited to see if her aunt would approve of her drive in the park. Clearly he assumed approval would not be a problem and, in the event, he was proved correct.

★ ★ ★

Amanda was relieved to find the day was turning out dry and mostly sunny, with only a few clouds drifting across the sky. Postponement of the outing to Hyde Park would have been very disappointing and she was keen to see what the daily parade was like.

Mr Mellor arrived promptly at four o'clock to find Amanda waiting and ready to go. Letitia said it was quite in order to make a gentleman wait a few minutes so as to not appear too eager, but Amanda saw no point in playing games with him.

'Good afternoon, Miss Buckley, may I carry your parasol for you?' he said at the open door.

'You may, Mr Mellor. I cannot see the point in bringing it, but my aunt insisted,' she said as they went down the steps.

'All the young ladies carry one, Miss Buckley. It is not only fashionable, but keeps the sun off their faces so they may retain their pale complexions,' he said as he assisted her into a curricle.

'Very well,' she said, as he climbed in on the other side, 'but I shall only carry it to be fashionable, since I have no pale complexion to worry about. I hardly think it necessary for me in this weak English sunshine, not even to keep cool.'

He studied her briefly as he set his horses into motion, but passed no comment.

'Does your groom not jump up

behind?' she asked.

'There is no need, I only brought him to hold the horses whilst I waited for you.'

'Oh, dear. In this case, I should have paid more attention to my cousin Letitia and let you wait a little. Your groom will think he served no purpose in coming.'

'Shame on your cousin,' he said with a chuckle, 'but it doesn't matter. My groom will be happy to sit around idly while he waits. Although, I wouldn't be surprised if he's already down the area steps and trying to get a snack of some sort from your kitchen.'

'Do we not need him for propriety's sake?' Amanda wasn't entirely sure of society rules and expected behaviour here in England.

'Oh, no, this is an open carriage and we will be visible at all times. I don't know how it is in India, but nobody here will pay any mind. Besides, I wanted to speak with you privately and I didn't want a servant with big ears standing behind us.'

'But surely we can't speak privately if

we are in a large procession in the park, can we?'

'There is nobody in the park I wish to speak to, so if you don't mind, I thought to drive a little further out around the park — but naturally we shall still be visible at all times.'

Amanda was somewhat dismayed, as she had wanted to see everything to do with the fashionable hour.

'Very well, but not too far away. I do wish to see the other carriages and who is driving in them. I was hoping you could tell me about them.'

'Of course, but all in good time. I wrote to my mother about you and she said she would dearly love to meet you, so I wondered if I could take you to meet her and my father, perhaps the day after tomorrow,' Mellor said as his horses trotted down Park Lane towards the park entrance.

'Yes, but . . . you wrote to her? So she is not here in London?'

'No, she is at our country estate just outside Henley. Her health is not very good, so she doesn't often come into London.'

Amanda's knowledge of English geography was still rather sketchy.

'Is it far from here?'

'About thirty miles, so we would need to make an early start.'

'For propriety I shall definitely have to take my maid, too, if we are going out of London, as well as seeking the approval of my aunt. This curricle will obviously not do, as it would be very uncomfortable for three of us to travel so far in it.'

'Yes, it would, and in any case I have only borrowed it and the groom from a friend of mine. I don't bother to keep my own carriage in London. I shall have to get a travelling carriage of some sort, as a chaise would be too small as well.'

Amanda only listened with half an ear to his descriptions of the other people in the park. She had been caught off-guard by the news his mother wanted to meet her. Wasn't this a little soon to be getting serious?

He was certainly handsome and amusing. He came from a titled family, but still, she wasn't sure how much she really liked him. On the other hand, she didn't feel especially welcome in her uncle's house and finding a husband before long would be convenient.

She definitely wasn't in love with Mr Mellor, but perhaps it might come when she knew him better. She thought some more about going to see his parents.

If they used a travelling carriage, Ramesh could ride on the back for good measure.

Would Aunt Viola approve of the expedition, especially as Amanda had only just met Mellor? And how well did her aunt know him? Presumably not very well, if he didn't know her cousins.

★ ★ ★

'Amanda says Mr Mellor's mother, the viscountess, has invited her to visit,' her aunt said to her uncle some time later. 'Apparently her health is not good and so

73

she wants Amanda to travel out to Henley or somewhere to visit her, instead of here in town.'

'Did she write to you? I don't recall a letter.'

'No. The invitation was through her son. What do you think, Henry? It all seems a trifle quick and irregular to me.'

'It is irregular, particularly when we hardly know these people. However, if we want someone to take her and those servants of hers off our hands, the sooner the better, eh?'

'I suppose so.'

'And she has already given me one hundred pounds for her keep this quarter, which is probably all we will ever get from her if she receives an offer soon.'

'If she does marry promptly, don't give any of it back. We will need it for some sort of wedding breakfast to wave her off.'

'I wouldn't dream of giving it back. No, it's all a bit odd, if you ask me, but she can go off to the Mellors' with my blessing.'

A Despicable Fortune Hunter

At eight o'clock in the morning, Amanda was waiting in the entrance hall with Debjani who was carrying a large carpet bag. Debjani had insisted on taking a few things in case the weather turned bad or Amanda needed to tidy herself before meeting the viscountess.

Minutes later, a carriage and pair with a postillion stopped at the house. Mellor opened the door and jumped down from the carriage. As Amanda and Debjani descended the house steps, he unfolded the carriage steps for them himself.

'Good morning, Miss Buckley, may I assist you?' he said, holding out a hand.

Debjani followed her inside while Ramesh emerged from the area steps and climbed on to the back step of the coach. As soon as everybody was aboard, Mellor called to the postillion to drive away.

'I'm afraid this hired carriage is not to the standard I would wish,' Mellor said, 'but I'm afraid this was all which was available at short notice.'

'I'm sure it will be adequate for a single day,' Amanda said, 'and I look forward to the journey, which will be my first expedition outside London since I arrived. You must tell me of any notable sights as we pass them.'

'Indeed I shall. Now, tell me, do you plan to set up your own carriage and horses?' Mellor asked.

Amanda looked at him with slight alarm. What was he supposing or suggesting? To set up her own stable and carriage was a costly business. She certainly wasn't going to reveal she could afford to do it.

She hadn't told anyone the size of her fortune, so was he suggesting this idea as a test to find out how much money she had?

Amanda knew she had to be on her guard against fortune hunters and was cautious about revealing her true circumstances. Besides, why would she want her own carriage in London? There was no point, except to show off.

If she was going to parade in the fashionable hour again in Hyde Park, it could be in someone else's carriage, just like two days ago, thank you very much.

'No, Mr Mellor, it's a very expensive thing to do and my uncle has his own vehicles which the ladies of the house can use should they have some requirement. There are not so many of us, so it is all we need. Apart from the occasional hackney,' she added, to be truthful, recalling her visit to the bank.

'You plan to reside in London, then?'

'For the time being, certainly, although I have heard much about Bath and Brighton . . . and York. I dare say it would be interesting to visit them sometime. However, for the moment I believe there are many interesting things to see and do in London.'

The weather was fair and promised to remain so all day. Their route was mostly along the busy Bath Road, which was in good condition.

Even so, the carriage was not very fast, being somewhat ancient and pulled by a single pair of horses. Several times they pulled to one side to let faster vehicles pass them.

Most of the morning passed as they rumbled along and various grand houses were pointed out to Amanda, such as Syon Park, Ditton Park and Windsor Castle in the distance. They stopped to change horses a couple of times, but the carriage wasn't very well sprung and the journey was becoming tiring. Amanda wasn't particularly looking forward to another three or four hours on the return trip.

It was a pity Mellor hadn't hired four horses, instead of a pair.

'Is it much farther, sir?' Amanda asked.

'It cannot be so very far off noon already.'

'There is an inn, the Rose and Crown, not too far ahead, where we may change the horses and stop for lunch. From there it will be not much further, perhaps just another ten miles.'

A little mental arithmetic told Amanda they should not linger over their lunch

78

and the visit to his mother would need to be quite short. Otherwise she would not arrive home before dark and then her aunt would worry. It seemed a lot of time and trouble for only a short visit to his mother.

Did he need his mother's approval to continue escorting Amanda? Perhaps he had mentioned Amanda's foreign looks to his mother, she was nervous about their association and wanted to take a look at Amanda herself before her son went any further.

The coach slowed and turned into the inn's yard. As it stopped, Ramesh jumped down and lowered the carriage steps. Mellor stepped down from the coach and then looked at him in surprise.

'Who are you? Don't tell me the Rose and Crown are employing Indian servants now,' he said.

'Oh, no,' Amanda said, following him down, 'he is my manservant and he is not Indian, he is Nepali.'

Ramesh bowed to Mellor before extending a hand to help Debjani down as well.

'He's a what? And where the devil did he spring from?' Mellor spluttered.

'The back of the coach, of course, unless you mean from somewhere in the Himalayas,' Amanda said with an impish grin.

Mellor looked confused and glanced at each of the three before recollecting himself.

'Come, I shall ask for a private parlour and a room where you may freshen up before lunch.'

Amanda and Debjani followed him into the inn, while Ramesh put the steps up again, before taking the bag and following them. As Ramesh reached the entrance, he stepped aside so Mellor could come back into the yard. Ramesh paused for a moment to see Mellor go and speak to the postillion, before Ramesh continued into the inn.

* * *

Amanda had gone up to a bedchamber to freshen up. When she came back down to the parlour, the table was laid for lunch, but Mellor was not there. He appeared moments later with a scowl on his face, which he quickly cleared when he saw Amanda was already at the table.

'My maid will join us for lunch for the sake of propriety,' Amanda said.

'Certainly. She may sit at the far end of the table,' he replied. 'May I help you to a little ham, Miss Buckley, or to the chicken?'

At the end of lunch, when the waiter had cleared the table and provided tea for the ladies and coffee for Mellor, he cleared his throat.

'We appear to have a slight problem, Miss Buckley. I went to check on the horses and postillion for the remainder of our journey. However, the postillion says he has only been paid to Maidenhead and for the return to London.

'He will not continue further on towards Henley unless I pay him what amounts to an extortionate amount of money. There is a change of horses available, but not another postillion to be had, but in any case he was hired with the carriage and will not leave it.'

'This is very annoying, isn't it? So have you paid him, despite his attempt at blackmail?'

'No, I'm afraid I cannot, I do not have so much money with me. I told him he would be paid on arrival in Henley, but he demanded payment in advance.'

'Oh. So what do you propose to do?'

'I wondered if you might lend me the money to pay him, which of course I will naturally refund as soon as we get back to London,' he said, looking suitably embarrassed.

'Me? But I have hardly any money, either. I brought just a little in case there were vails to be paid, but nothing more.'

His embarrassment changed into puzzlement.

'But surely a wealthy lady such as yourself would carry much more than this?'

'I? Wealthy? What gives you the idea I

am wealthy?'

Now Mellor was completely taken aback and he blinked in surprise as he stared at her.

'Because it is common knowledge. Everybody knows your father was a nabob and you are his only child and heir.'

'Who has said so? I have never said my father was a nabob. It seems to me, Mr Mellor, it is not so much common knowledge as common speculation.'

'But your aunt said you were a rich heiress.'

'Did she, indeed? I have no idea why she would say this.' In fact Amanda had a strong suspicion of why she would say it. She was fairly sure her aunt would be glad to be rid of her when she had two rather dowdy and dull-witted daughters to marry off. Claiming Amanda to be a rich heiress would no doubt stimulate interest, with a view to an early marriage. It was not an idea which would endear Amanda to her aunt when she was particularly trying to avoid fortune hunters due to her father's warning.

'I expect she said it because your uncle told her so.'

'I pay my uncle one hundred pounds a quarter as my contribution to the household expenses. He knows this is half my quarterly allowance, so why do you suppose he thinks I am a rich heiress?'

Mellor's jaw dropped and he stared at her in horror.

'You have . . . only eight hundred pounds a year? But this is nothing, I thought . . .'

'It may be nothing to you, but many people could live quite comfortably on eight hundred a year. Not extravagantly, perhaps, but certainly adequately and in comfort.'

Amanda looked at him without sympathy. She should have realised before, he was nothing but a fortune hunter. So much for his sweet words. He was exactly the sort of person she had been hoping to avoid.

Furthermore, it was clearly her aunt and uncle's doing. Mr Mellor's hurry for her to meet his parents was explained now. She had no desire to be the bird in his hand. Her father's warning echoed in her mind. How could she have been so stupid as to not see it all before?

Mellor rested his elbows on the table and covered his face with his hands.

'But, but . . . ' he said. 'Oh, what a fool I have been.'

Amanda thought this was true of both of them. He looked up in obvious despair.

'I have been tricked! Tricked!'

'Not by me, Mr Mellor.'

'Perhaps not, but certainly by your family. Surely you realise marrying you is out of the question unless you are wealthy?'

'And why is that, sir?' Amanda said in an icy voice.

'Because we have no money! We could only overlook your unfortunate appearance if you brought us money. I think you are quite pretty in a foreign sort of way, but without money you simply will not do.'

Amanda rose to her feet and he stood automatically, too. She put her hands on the table and leaned towards him.

'You, Mr Mellor, are the deceiver!' she said in a loud and angry voice. 'You pretend to be my admirer, but all you admire is money. I do not consider my skin colour to be unfortunate compared to the insipid pale girls you obviously prefer. Never mind referring to what you call my foreign prettiness.

'You, sir, are a snake in the grass and nothing more than a despicable and deceitful fortune hunter whom I have no wish to ever see again.'

'Nor I you, Miss Buckley, nor any of your family again — especially your two ugly cousins!'

'Get out!' Amanda said, pointing a trembling finger at the open doorway, at which was standing a scowling Ramesh.

'May I kill him for you, Misa Amanda?' Ramesh asked, with his hand upon his kukri.

'No, Ramesh, do not soil your hands. Let him go.'

Ramesh stood to the side. Mellor looked at him fearfully, before running out of the door. They heard his feet clattering hurriedly down the stairs and a distant door slam. Ramesh closed the parlour door and leaned back on it with his arms crossed.

Debjani moved to a trembling Amanda and put a cup of tea in front of her.

'Drink your tea, Misa Amanda. It is as well you discovered he was a good-for-nothing before you became any more involved.'

Debjani handed Amanda a handkerchief to dry the tears rolling down her cheeks.

A few minutes later there was the noise of a carriage rolling out of the yard. Ramesh crossed to the window.

'The devil! He has gone, but has taken the carriage with him,' he said.

Amanda and Debjani looked at each other.

'Oh, misa, what shall we do now?' Debjani asked, voicing what they were both thinking.

'I have to write to my uncle and ask him to come and collect us. Go downstairs and ask for writing materials. Ask the landlady to come upstairs as well.' Amanda was in no mood to speak to another man.

★ ★ ★

'Yes, miss, how may I help you?' the rather plump landlady asked in a very friendly voice and Amanda relaxed a little.

'I shall be staying here tonight, so require a room for myself with a truckle bed for my maid and an adjoining room for my manservant.'

'Very good, miss, just the one night?'

'Yes, I expect so, although possibly two. The man who brought me turned out to be dishonest and brought me here under false pretences. He has gone off now with a flea in his ear and taken the carriage with him. I don't expect to see him again.

'As a result I need to send a note to my uncle in London and ask him to come and collect me. I can't be sure if he will arrive tomorrow or the day after.'

'Bless you, dear, you're better off without a deceitful young man, even if he was very pretty. We have a bedchamber with a small sitting-room which has a second adjoining bedchamber, too, if it would suit you.'

'Yes, thank you, it will do quite nicely.'

The landlady smiled.

'Very good, miss. You stay right here with us in the Rose and Crown where you'll be comfortable and write your letter. I'm sure you don't want to go to London on the stage or the mail, because they're crowded and smelly. Not the sort of thing for a young lady like you.

'When your letter is done, you send it downstairs and the boy can run down to the Bell with it, because that's where the mail coach stops.' The landlady stood aside as a waiter carried in a writing box and placed it on the table. Then she bobbed a curtsey and followed the waiter out.

The letter written and sent downstairs, Amanda wondered what to do in the meantime. She regretted not having brought a book, but she hadn't thought there would be any occasion to read one.

'Debjani, would you go and ask the landlady if there are any reading books I could borrow?'

Debjani soon returned.

'The landlady sends her apologies, but they don't have any books to lend you. It doesn't surprise me, because it doesn't look the sort of place where much reading happens.

'There's plenty of talk in the public bar, but they're all men and look to me like farmers. I could barely understand their accent either while I was waiting for the landlady.'

Amanda wondered if she was their topic of discussion — not that she could do anything about it, and it didn't really matter anyway. However, she intended to stay well out of sight until Uncle Henry or his travelling coach arrived. She had no desire to rouse speculation of any kind.

In the meantime, she decided to go to

her bedchamber and have a rest while she thought about everything. Who else among her recent dance partners might be fortune hunters too? She felt sure she could at least acquit young Mr Seaton of any such base motives.

After the early start in Wimpole Street, the long journey, the argument and the anxiety, it wasn't long before she fell asleep.

Debjani sat in an armchair in the sittingroom and took a little sewing from her bag to occupy the time. Ramesh sat watchfully in another chair.

In a little while, there was a knock at the door. Ramesh opened it and stood blocking the entrance, so they couldn't come in and make noise to disturb his mistress. The landlady was there with a gentleman dressed in riding gear. He said he wanted to speak to Miss Amanda.

'No,' Ramesh said curtly. Ramesh didn't care who he was, and if word had got around about a single lady being left behind in this inn, this person might have the wrong idea of what kind of lady she was.

Wanted to assist her, did he? They didn't need assistance of any kind, especially if this man thought he could take advantage of a single lady on her own. No, he could take himself off. Whoever he said he was, he was not coming into Misa Amanda's rooms. Ramesh stood there, glaring at the man until the man got the message and went away.

However, the quiet talking next door was enough to rouse Amanda from her light nap.

'Who was it, Ramesh?' she called.

'He said he was the Earl of Twyford and wanted to speak to you.'

'I don't know any earls and why would he want to speak with me?'

'I could not think of any good reasons nor why he might be here, so I sent him away.' Ramesh didn't want to voice any of his own speculation about the man and his motives.

Amanda climbed from the bed and went to the window to see if there was anything worth looking at.

As she looked out, there was a man mounting his horse before wheeling it to the exit of the inn yard. As he turned, a handsome face glanced up at her and she stepped back from the window with a sharp breath.

A Light-Hearted Wager

'If you've finished your breakfast, shall we go to the Rose and Crown and see if you can discover who the mysterious lady is?' Edmund asked.

'Yes; give me a few minutes while I dress for going out,' his sister Geraldine said. 'I am supposing the footman left the books there with the mystery lady and didn't bring them back last night?'

'I imagine so. Obviously they weren't handed to you when he came back and the butler passed no comment to me about them.'

They were soon trotting down the drive in Edmund's curricle.

'I must say this is vastly entertaining,' Geraldine said, 'it was getting a little dull at home with hardly any visitors.'

'Don't you worry, we shall go to London before long and then you will soon be worn out by the constant round of parties and balls.'

'Oh, yes, please! I confess I am looking

forward to meeting lots and lots of handsome young men eager to dance with me.'

'Oh, I don't think you need to worry on that score.'

Geraldine sat back with a little smile on her face. She was looking forward to some entertainment in London. Then her thoughts turned towards the mystery guest at the Rose and Crown.

'Do you suppose this lady at the inn will be rich, beautiful and looking for a husband?' she said, grinning at her brother.

Edmund chuckled.

'Your flights of fancy are always entertaining. No, I think it improbable. I think it more likely she is a middle-aged widow, lately arrived from India. I'm guessing India because of the appearance of her manservant.

'Then, in addition, she can't be very old if she was writing to an uncle and she can't be very young either if she is there on her own. Middle-aged is my strong expectation, also because she is travelling with her own servants, which implies she has her own household.

'Who the gentleman in whose company she arrived might be, I haven't the faintest idea. However, I am very curious to know who she is.'

'Are you sure she is respectable?'

'Mr Thomas thought she was, but couldn't be sure. When you see her, you must make your own judgement. If you have any suspicion she is not a proper person for us to know, you must make your excuses and leave at once. There is a certain class of person with whom neither of us should associate.'

'I expect we shall soon find out. If I am right and she is young, beautiful and looking for a husband, you have to buy me a new bonnet. If you are right and she is a middle-aged widow, I shall buy new hat for you instead,' Geraldine said.

'You forgot to say she should be rich, too. But very well, it is a wager, just provided you don't force me to marry the lady as part of the bargain.'

'If I am getting a new bonnet, you

ought to be getting one for your wife, too. It's past time you married, you know. I hope to find myself a husband in the approaching season and if you don't find yourself a wife soon, you will dwindle into a reclusive old bachelor, which will never do.'

'No, I agree,' Edmund said, sobering. 'I dread to think of cousin Cedric inheriting the title. I suppose I will have to do something about the succession before long. However, I have yet to meet anyone interesting enough to want to spend the rest of my life with them. A marriage of convenience is far from appealing.'

They turned into the yard of the inn. Edmund tossed the reins to an ostler who came running up, while Geraldine jumped down without waiting for her brother to help her. As they walked into the inn, the landlord came to greet them.

'Good morning, Mr Thomas,' Edmund said, 'I trust your mysterious guests are still here?'

'Oh, yes, my lord, we have just this moment cleared away their breakfast things from the parlour.'

'Excellent. Would you ask your good wife to escort Lady Geraldine up there? In the meantime I will take coffee in the tap room.'

'Of course, sir,' the landlord said and opened the door to the kitchen. 'Doris, come out here, please, and take Lady Geraldine up to see Miss Buckley.'

'Miss Buckley,' Edmund mouthed silently to his sister with a knowing nod. She waved an admonishing finger at him and silently mouthed 'Not a widow' back at him. She grinned and tapped him playfully on the arm. He shrugged.

'Good morning, my lady,' Doris said, emerging from the back, wiping her hands on an apron and then bobbing a curtsey. 'Would you follow me, please?'

'Geraldine, if you're not back down by the time I've finished my coffee, I shall walk into town and come back to collect you at noon.'

Geraldine nodded at him, before following the landlady, while Edmund headed for one of the tables in the taproom.

Upstairs, the landlady tapped on the sitting-room door and Ramesh appeared in the opening.

'Lady Geraldine Nisbet to see Miss Buckley,' the landlady said.

'Please come in,' a lady's voice said and Ramesh opened the door wide. Geraldine stepped in, then stopped in surprise.

Miss Buckley had coffee-coloured skin, glossy hair and was exotically beautiful. Geraldine smiled broadly at this lady who could not be much older than herself. Oh, yes! Edmund was surely going to owe her a new bonnet.

Someone knocked at the door and Amanda looked up from her book.

'Lady Geraldine Nisbet,' she heard the landlady say. Oh. This was the nice lady who had loaned her the books. Amanda hoped the kind gesture meant she might be friendly. Based on her recent experiences, there was no way to know, and it was entirely possible she might want the books back at once, when she had seen Amanda.

Ramesh stood aside and she could see

this Lady Geraldine was much younger than Amanda had guessed. She looked very English, with blonde hair swept back into a bun and a couple of ringlets framing her face. She also looked shocked, which wasn't very promising. Then a pleased smile crossed her face and she stepped forward. Amanda sagged with relief.

'Miss Buckley, I am so very pleased to meet you,' Geraldine said, and they both curtseyed.

'Lady Geraldine, thank you for calling and for the loan of the books. Would you care for tea?'

'Yes, thank you,' Geraldine said, and Amanda nodded to Ramesh.

'I've been sitting at home with nothing to do, so when I heard you were stranded here, I thought to come and see if I could be of assistance. If nothing else, it would be refreshing to talk to somebody new.'

'I'm glad you came, and for the books, without which it would be very tedious waiting here. As it is, they are very entertaining.'

'I thought so too, especially the second one, 'Pride and Prejudice', which is . . . ' Geraldine paused when Amanda held up her hand.

'You mustn't tell me what happens, I'm still reading the first book!'

'Oh, of course, I'm so sorry, I wouldn't want to spoil it for you. How do you like the first one so far?'

'Very well, although it has echoes of my own situation, as I've had to leave my home and move far away to a place where I don't know anybody.'

'Oh, dear. Has your father died, too, and a stepbrother pushed you out as well?'

'No, not quite. My parents died and my father wished me to leave Calcutta and come to live in London with my uncle and his family. He is Baron Walsh and they live in Wimpole Street in London.

'My mother's family are Bengalis and live in Calcutta, but it would have been awkward for everybody had I gone to live with them instead. I doubt they would have known quite what to do with me.'

'Ah. I don't wish to be indelicate, but is this why you have . . . Indian features?'

'Yes, my father was English, but my mother was a Bengali. Do you mind?'

'Mind? No, why should I mind?'

'It seems many people do. My uncle and aunt are uncomfortable around my servants too. Especially Ramesh, my man-servant.'

Geraldine sneaked a look behind herself to see if Ramesh was still there, and then laughed.

'Well, you must admit your manservant looks very fierce and intimidating!'

Amanda laughed as well.

'Yes, he does, doesn't he? My father insisted he come with me for my protection and Ramesh takes the idea very seriously. He even swore an oath to my father that he would guard me with his life. He is very loyal and honourable and I have no doubt he really meant it. If nothing else, he certainly knows how to frighten people.'

'It must be very reassuring to have such a guard, but what brings you to the

Rose and Crown? And what is this tale I heard of a pretty young man bringing you here and then abandoning you?'

'Oh, the abominable Mr Mellor. Yes, the very picture of a handsome young man about town. He seemed to be courting me and brought me here on the way to meet his mother. Everything was happening very quickly and I should have been suspicious. It now appears he thought I was wealthy and was only interested in my money. A fortune hunter.

'When he learned the story of my wealth was pure speculation, he got very angry and insulting and went off on his own with the carriage, leaving me here. The carriage was hired, so I am supposing he is virtually penniless and as a result was determined to court a rich heiress.'

'What a scoundrel and an unscrupulous self-serving villain as well!' Geraldine exclaimed. 'It sounds as if you were lucky to find out sooner rather than later.'

'Yes. A complete snake in the grass. However, now I have to wait here for my uncle to send someone to collect me, because I didn't bring enough money to hire another carriage.'

'Why don't you come and stay with us instead of waiting here?'

'It is kind of you, but I ought to wait here so my uncle or his coachman can find me. I expect he will be annoyed enough with me as it is, so I shouldn't go elsewhere. What shall I do with your books when he comes?'

'Oh, you can leave them here. The landlord knows us well. Or you can simply keep them and send them to me when you have finished them.'

'You are well known here?'

'Oh, yes. The Rose and Crown is part of the Twyford Estate, so my brother actually owns the inn. Besides, Twyford Hall is only a mile away and everybody knows us hereabouts.'

'Your brother is the Earl of Twyford?'

'Yes, the landlord told him about your predicament yesterday.'

'I'm so sorry. We didn't know who he was or what he wanted, so Ramesh sent him away. After the episode with Mr Mellor, we suspected your brother's motives for asking if we wanted help. I shall be so embarrassed to meet him now. Please apologise on my behalf.'

There was knock at the door. Ramesh opened it to find a waiter there.

'Excuse me, Lady Geraldine, but his lordship says he is downstairs and waiting for you.'

'Thank you,' Geraldine said. 'Goodness me, is it noon already? I must leave now, Miss Buckley, but it has been a real pleasure to meet you. We will probably stop by tomorrow to make sure your uncle has found you and taken you home.'

Amanda squeezed Geraldine's hands.

'I have been pleased to meet you, too. Perhaps I will see you in London?'

'My brother says we shall be going there soon and I think Brook Street is quite close to Wimpole Street, so I will be happy to call on you,' Geraldine said.

Ramesh held the door for her as she headed downstairs.

'She seems like a nice lady,' Debjani said, as the door closed behind Geraldine, 'and not with funny ideas like your cousins.'

'Yes, she is, and it's refreshing to meet someone who doesn't regard us with suspicion simply because of our appearance.'

'And she was friendly, too. Lady Geraldine strikes me as an intelligent young lady as well as being an engaging person.'

'I agree. I shall look forward to meeting her again when we are back in London.'

* * *

'So, sister, tell me about the mysterious Miss Buckley,' Edmund said as they jogged home in his curricle.

'She's not rich but she is young, only a little older than me I think. She has slightly Indian features, is outstandingly beautiful and not married. I think you will owe me a hat.'

'Not so fast. You said before she had to be rich and looking for a husband.'

'She's young and not married, so it's much the same thing. Not only this, but she was brought here by a man whom she thought was courting her.

'He had the wickedness to abandon her here when he discovered she wasn't the rich heiress he had supposed. Now she has to wait for her uncle to collect her.'

'I see, so not rich, but I do see what you mean. If she thought she was being courted, then perhaps she actually is looking for a husband. By the sound of it, and she really is as beautiful as you say, she probably won't have much difficulty finding someone else to marry. I still don't think it's a hat.'

'Not so fast, not so fast! She has servants and, in particular, if her dress is anything to go by, she's not a pauper, either. Not many ladies wear day dresses which are of a very fine silk — they generally keep such good silks for evening wear.'

'A fine silk for day wear? Is that so? Then is it her uncle who is wealthy?'

'I don't know. He is Baron Walsh and they live in Wimpole Street.'

'Hmm. I don't know him and it's not the best address, so he's probably not particularly wealthy. How is it, then, she's expensively dressed and yet not wealthy? Is he really her uncle? Are you sure she's entirely respectable?'

'Quite sure. I think she said she had only recently gone to live with her uncle.'

'Ah. In this case, where has she come from?'

'Calcutta.'

'Calcutta? Oh, well, that explains everything: the features, the uncle and the servants. Also, I don't doubt silk dresses are less expensive in India. Very well, I shall reserve judgement on the hat and, in any case, I'm sure you will prefer to visit a milliner in Bond Street, rather than Maidenhead.'

'I invited her to come and stay with us while she waited for her uncle, but she declined. I hope you don't mind me offering?'

'No, I don't mind. We have plenty of space and a visitor would enliven things for you. I realise it must be a bit dull for you here on your own in the country when everybody else has moved to town. I promise I will finish my business as soon as I can, then we can go to London too.'

'Next time we meet, I shall tell her what a kind and handsome brother I have.'

'Next time?'

'We must come back tomorrow to see if her uncle has succeeded in rescuing her and if she has left my books behind for me to collect. If she is not still here, I intend calling upon her in Wimpole Street.

'Mind you, if she is still here tomorrow, I definitely think I should introduce you. You probably think I am exaggerating wildly about her beauty.'

Edmund glanced at her with a raised eyebrow, but refrained from comment.

A Cruel Rejection

'Why, dear sister, are you subjecting me to this inspection? Do you suppose my valet is failing in his duties?'

Geraldine had stopped him as they were about to leave home and was now carefully looking him over. Geraldine thought Miss Buckley might have potential as the next Countess of Twyford, so she considered it important he make a good first impression.

'Not at all, dear brother, I simply feel you should look your best when visiting a lady.'

Geraldine was of the firm opinion her brother really needed to find himself a wife who would keep him up to the mark. She was ready to find herself a husband, but she didn't feel she could focus on the task while she thought her brother needed her to maintain their standards. He needed a wife so she could have some independence.

Edmund sighed. He could see what his sister was thinking.

'I could get very irritated if you take it into your head to do some matchmaking. I'm quite capable of finding a wife myself. Just because I haven't found the right one so far, doesn't mean I don't wish to.

'Besides, for all we know, her uncle has collected her and she is on her way home to Mayfair.'

'All you say is true,' Geraldine said, twitching his neckcloth to be perfectly straight. 'However, if your appearance is too casual when escorting your sister, it speaks of disrespect.'

Edmund rolled his eyes at her fussing, as she then stepped back and looked at him critically, before nodding to herself.

'You'll do,' she said. 'Come along, don't dawdle.'

As they went out to his curricle, Edmund hoped his eventual wife would be more easy-going. If Geraldine would only find herself a husband, she could concentrate on him and then leave her brother in peace. He hadn't properly understood why his sister hadn't made a push to find herself a husband.

Arriving at the inn, they enquired and were told Miss Buckley was still there. Edmund headed for a table, calling for coffee, while Geraldine headed upstairs without waiting for a servant to conduct her. She tapped at the door and it was opened promptly by Ramesh. He immediately stood aside.

'Misa Amanda, Lady Geraldine is here to see you,' he called over his shoulder.

Geraldine stepped into the sitting-room and came to a halt in surprise. Miss Buckley was coming towards her with red eyes and outstretched hands.

'Whatever has happened, Miss Buckley?' she said, taking Amanda's hands. Amanda burst into tears, obviously not for the first time, so Geraldine pulled her into a hug.

After a minute or two the tears subsided and Geraldine sat Amanda in one of the armchairs and knelt beside her.

'Miss Buckley,' she said, 'tell me what is wrong and let me help you.'

'My uncle has cast me off,' Amanda

sobbed. 'Now what am I to do? Look.'
She handed a letter to Geraldine.

Miss Buckley,
Lady Walsh and I are disappointed
and shocked at your departure in the
company of Mr Mellor on the pre-
text of visiting his mother. We had
expected your return before night-
fall.

As you have chosen instead to
spend the night at a common inn,
you must realise your reputation is
destroyed beyond redemption.

As a consequence, we can no
longer welcome you into our home,
as the reputation of my entire family, especially my two daughters,
would be ruined by association.

As you have chosen a different
path, you must now follow it on your
own without any communication or
acknowledgement from ourselves.

Yours sincerely,
Henry, Baron Walsh.

'Oh! How heartless and unfeeling,' Geraldine said, 'as if you had deliberately engineered the situation when it was all Mellor's fault, not yours.'

'I think he has seized on an opportunity to get rid of me,' Amanda said, another tear rolling down her cheek.

'Get rid of you? Why should he want to get rid of you?'

'Because I'm half Indian, he doesn't like my servants and I didn't bring him a lot of money, either. He and my father didn't get on well together and then my father didn't leave him anything in his will as perhaps my uncle expected.

'As a result, he no doubt he saw me as an embarrassment and a liability, so wanted me to disappear. He has now seized the opportunity to dispose of me.'

'I think it is perfectly horrible and if I meet him I shall give him the cut direct. Never mind, you shall come and stay with us as my guest and you will be very welcome in our house.'

'Oh, it is very kind of you, but I wouldn't want to inconvenience you and your brother.'

'There is no inconvenience. He will be glad of me keeping you company and leaving him in peace.'

'Lady Geraldine, this is very kind of you and perhaps the inn won't press me to pay my bill for a few days if I am staying locally.

'I didn't even think to bring enough money to pay my reckoning here. It is horribly awkward and humiliating. I shall have to send to my bank in London for the money to pay them which will take a day or so.'

'Hush! It is Edmund's inn and he will simply tell the landlord to send the bill to him.'

'Oh, no. Then I will be in debt to your brother like a poor relation asking for charity. It is very demeaning and distressing.'

'Nonsense! Edmund is a very kind and generous man and will be pleased to help you. He is sufficiently wealthy not even to notice the amount. He is downstairs and I will go to fetch him so you may see for yourself. He is very indulgent towards me and undoubtedly will be towards my new friend as well.

'Debjani,' she said, turning to the maid, 'bathe your mistress's eyes in cold water and then dry her face. Perhaps a little rice powder, too?' Then Geraldine had second thoughts, pursed her lips and looked at Amanda's face. Miss Buckley had a coffee coloured complexion and white rice powder would look very odd upon it.

'No, no, not rice powder, how silly of me. Er . . . I leave it up to you, Debjani, I'm sure you know best what to do. I shall be gone for at least five minutes, so you may have a little time to restore Miss Buckley's appearance.' She patted Amanda's hand. 'Fear not, all will be well and I will be back shortly.'

Geraldine hurried downstairs and joined Edmund at his table. He folded the newspaper which he had been browsing.

'Edmund, it is an altogether shocking thing,' she said quietly, to not attract the attention of others in the tap room. 'Her uncle has cast her off, all because this Mr Mellor abandoned her here overnight and now her uncle says her reputation is ruined.

'This is despite her maid being with her all the time and her footman here, too, to shield them both from unwanted attention. She thinks her uncle is glad to be rid of her because she looks Indian and didn't bring lots of money to line his pockets.'

'How completely disgraceful. I mean both Mellor, whoever he is, and her uncle, too. Who did you say her uncle was?'

'Baron Walsh. From his letter, I gather he has a wife and two daughters. It wouldn't surprise me if the daughters are both antidotes who are cast into the shade by their cousin.'

'Maybe so, but it doesn't excuse his behaviour. As for Mellor, I think if I come across him I might take him into a quiet corner and demonstrate what happens to gentlemen who act dishonourably.'

'Good. I'm glad to hear it. In the meantime, I have invited Miss Buckley to come and stay with us until she can decide what to do next. Are you sure you don't mind?'

'Of course not, I trust your judgement in this since you have spent time with the lady and have no doubt formed a good opinion of her.'

'She is also distressed about not having brought enough money with her to pay the bill. Naturally she expected first Mellor and then her uncle to pay it.'

'She need not be embarrassed. I shall speak to Mr Thomas and ask him to give me the bill.'

'Excellent, I knew I could rely on you. See Mr Thomas, and then come upstairs with me, because you absolutely must meet her right now.'

Edmund finished his coffee and went to have a word with Mr Thomas the landlord. Then he followed Geraldine upstairs. Geraldine tapped on the sitting-room door, then simply walked in, followed by Edmund.

'Edmund, this is Miss Buckley,' she said, 'Miss Buckley, this is my brother Edmund, the Earl of Twyford.'

Amanda had been half expecting the earl to be a male version of his sister, but he wasn't. Where Lady Geraldine had straw blonde hair, his was darker.

Then there was nothing remotely feminine about him, unlike the infamous Mr Mellor, and he was at least a head taller than everyone else in the room. He was also staring in surprise at Amanda for an exceedingly long moment before blinking and bowing to her.

At his first sight of Amanda, Edmund was stunned and frozen to the spot while she curtseyed to him. Geraldine had said the lady was beautiful, but for once in her life, his sister had understated the matter. Her eyes! She had the most beautiful eyes he had ever seen, framed by long lashes, dark eyebrows and high cheekbones.

Her shining hair framed a heart-shaped face. He blinked twice, came to himself once more and bowed, somewhat belatedly.

'Miss Buckley, I am pleased to meet you at last. Geraldine has spoken highly of you. We will be delighted to have you as our guest while you decide upon your future plans.'

'My lord, this is very kind of you and I am extremely grateful for your assistance. I apologise for my manservant turning you away before, but you were quite unknown to me.'

Edmund waved the apology away dismissively.

'Not at all. I am glad you are so well protected.' He nodded to Ramesh who was standing impassively in a corner. Ramesh inclined his head in acknowledgement.

'May I suggest,' Edmund continued, 'Geraldine and I return home in my curricle. The housekeeper can then be preparing a room for you while you pack your things here. We will return very soon in my travelling carriage to collect you all.'

'Thank you, my lord, I also have a slight problem with my bill here . . . '

Edmund waved it away with a smile.

'I have already spoken to the landlord and he will forward the bill to my secretary tomorrow, so do not concern yourself about it today.'

'Thank you, my lord, I am very relieved to be rescued from such a difficult situation.'

'Not at all. We will see you again shortly. Shall we go?' he said to Geraldine.

'Edmund, you go ahead and I'll stay here with Miss Buckley until you return. You don't need me to speak to the housekeeper.'

He nodded agreement and went downstairs to find his curricle, then head home.

Geraldine thought to stay with Miss Buckley in case she needed further reassurance or if she needed to speak about clothing, not having planned a stay here.

'Well, Miss Buckley, did I not say my brother was kind and generous?'

'You did, Lady Geraldine, and I consider myself lucky to have met you both.'

'If we are to be friends, and I do hope

we will, you must call me simply Geraldine and my brother Edmund.'

'Then you must call me Amanda. I shall be pleased to call you Geraldine, but it seems rather presumptuous to call his lordship by his first name when I have only met him the once.'

'Well, we shall see. In the meantime, I am guessing you may be short of clothing as you did not expect an overnight stop. I think we are much the same size, so when we arrive home we shall set our maids to see what there is of mine which I can lend you.'

'Geraldine, your kindness is overwhelming. I don't know how I shall ever repay you both.'

'I'm sure we'll find a way,' Geraldine said, with a rather knowing smile.

'Tomorrow, do you suppose his lordship would lend me the travelling carriage?'

'I hope you're not planning to leave so soon!'

'No, no, but I would like to send Ramesh and Debjani to my uncle's house to collect all my belongings. I have a number of trunks there which I would like to remove before my uncle takes it into his head to investigate the contents. And at the same time, Debjani can collect my clothing before my aunt has it re-made to fit my cousins.'

'Do you think they would do such a thing?' a shocked Geraldine asked.

'I wouldn't put it past them. My uncle seems rather grasping and now they have thrown me out, they may conclude anything which I have left behind becomes theirs.'

'In this case, shouldn't they go today, before your uncle and aunt reach this conclusion?'

'Perhaps they should, to collect everything of mine before anyone there has thought of taking it. I would not like to lose my keepsakes or jewellery.'

Edmund was back within the hour with the carriage. While they were travelling the short distance back to Twyford Hall, Geraldine explained Amanda's concerns about her possessions.

'I agree,' Edmund said. 'It sounds as if Baron Walsh is unscrupulous and I think it wise to go immediately. As soon as we arrive home, the carriage can take your servants to his house without delay to retrieve your belongings.

'If they leave immediately they can be there before four o'clock. Say an hour to load everything and they can be back by nine when it will still be light. I think, for good measure, I will send two, no, three, of my footmen as well.'

'Amanda, do you have a lot of baggage?' Geraldine asked.

'Half a dozen large trunks and various other bags. I'm sure Ramesh and Debjani will be able manage even if my uncle's servants won't help.'

'Perhaps I am being pessimistic,' Edmund said, 'but I thought to avoid any argument or debate in Wimpole Street. If the fearsome Ramesh appears on their doorstep with three strong liveried footmen behind him, I don't expect anyone will stand in their way.'

'Oh. I had not considered opposition,'

Amanda said, 'but I see your point. Before they set off, I shall write a brief note to say I am staying as Lady Geraldine's guest. I don't know if they will care, but it seems the civil thing to do.

'I must write another for Ramesh to take to my bank while he is in London, so I have some money and they have my new direction as well.'

'Good. While you are doing this, I will tell the stables to add another pair of horses to the carriage and to the coachman to make good speed. He can change horses at Colnbrook and then collect mine on the way back.'

'Thank you for this, my lord,' Amanda said, smiling at him, 'I appreciate the effort you are making on my behalf and how it must be a great inconvenience to you.'

'Not at all, Miss Buckley, it is merely a question of doing what is right and proper.' Not only did Edmund consider it right and proper, he thought it would be difficult to refuse her anything when she smiled at him like that.

The servants arrived in Wimpole Street shortly after four o'clock, despite a short deviation to the bank in Fleet Street. Ramesh rapped the knocker vigorously, while the footmen and Debjani stood behind him. The door opened to reveal Mr Keith, the butler, whose eyes opened wide to see Ramesh and a small crowd of servants standing behind him.

'We have come to collect Miss Buckley's belongings,' Ramesh said.

'Go down to the servants' entrance and wait while I inform his lordship,' Mr Keith said, as he started to close the door.

'We will not wait,' Ramesh said, scowling at him. He pushed the door wide and walked in. 'However, you may inform his lordship if you wish, giving him this letter at the same time.' He handed Amanda's letter to Mr Keith and then strode past him. The five of them headed up the main staircase.

'Here, you can't do that, you have to

use the servants' stairs,' the butler spluttered.

Ramesh ignored him. The others followed his lead. A few minutes later Ramesh and the footmen came back down, two at a time, each pair carrying a trunk between them. The butler tried to bar their way, but they simply pushed past him.

'You can't take those away without the master's permission,' he shouted to absolutely no effect.

Other servants started to appear in the hallway to find out what was going on. Having put the trunks in the carriage, the men came back in and headed up the stairs once more. The next time they came back down with two more trunks, the butler and a couple of the baron's footmen tried to block their path.

Ramesh snarled at them in a menacing way. The footmen leapt out of his way and even Mr Keith stepped back, too. The next time they came downstairs with the last two trunks followed by Debjani carrying several bags.

This time Lady Walsh was there.

'How dare you!' she exclaimed. 'You have no right to take these things.'

Ramesh paused.

'These are my mistress's belongings and she has instructed me to collect them,' he said to her.

'You are an impudent heathen,' Lady Walsh said, 'and I shall have you dismissed for this.'

'No, milady,' he said with a broad smile, 'I am an impudent Christian and you cannot dismiss me because you have no authority over me. Good day to you.'

What Does the Future Hold?

Edmund entered the breakfast-room to find the two ladies already there. Now the crisis had abated, he thought Miss Buckley was sitting at his table looking entirely relaxed and entirely beautiful, too. Her dress was an especially fine and brightly coloured muslin which contrasted so well with her dark features. She and his blonde, blue-eyed sister made a perfect foil for each other. Geraldine was looking very pleased with herself this morning.

'Good morning, Miss Buckley. Good morning, Geraldine. Did you sleep well, Miss Buckley?'

'Yes, thank you, my lord, the room is very comfortable and it was convenient to have all my things to hand before I retired.'

'Good. Did you receive all of your possessions and were they in a proper condition?'

'A couple of the trunks looked as if

someone had tried to force them open, but failed. The locks are sturdy, but it is just as well we retrieved them before a locksmith could be called.'

'Yes, indeed. I'm glad we retrieved them in time and I am saddened they tried to open them. Next week we shall go to London and I will be mentioning their behaviour to my friends. They can't do this sort of thing and get away with it.'

'I wouldn't wish to cause you more trouble, my lord.'

He smiled reassuringly at her. The only trouble she was likely to cause him was for him to forget whatever else it was he was supposed to be doing today.

'Don't you worry about it. My reputation is quite secure and I am confident people will entirely believe whatever I may say. No, Baron Walsh will be sorry he crossed us.

'I hear from my footmen that your manservant Ramesh simply strode in and claimed your belongings in the face of protest from their servants. My men were very impressed by the way he did it.'

'Oh, yes, I heard all about it from my maid. She said Lady Walsh threatened him with dismissal, but he just laughed at her and said it was beyond her power. By all accounts they left while she was still screaming at them and all the neighbours were watching what was going on.'

'I do hope they noticed my crest on the doors of the carriage and noted we are not friends of Baron Walsh.'

'Oh. I wonder if, now she has had time for reflection, she realises it was foolish to stand in the street hurling abuse?'

Edmund smiled wryly.

'I imagine if you have more gowns like the ones you have been wearing, she no doubt had been hoping to acquire them for her daughters. Instead, she must have been frustrated at losing all of them. By all accounts, it serves her right.'

'Oh, Edmund, you should see Amanda's wardrobe, she has the most wonderful dresses and shawls.'

'No doubt, Geraldine, I shall see them progressively as the days pass.' He instantly realised he really was looking forward to seeing Miss Buckley each day, never mind what dresses she was wearing.

'In fact, if Miss Buckley is a connoisseuse of silks, as I suspect she may be, then once we are in London, a tour of the silk warehouses may be in order.'

'Do you think we could?' Geraldine asked, sounding excited.

'I should be delighted,' Amanda said. 'I have notes from my father of the names of the best importers. I'm sure they will be happy to show us around.'

'There you are, dear sister,' Edmund said, 'you might even find something suitable for that new bonnet you are hoping to receive.'

She grinned at him and then couldn't help a thoughtful glance at Amanda.

'Shall we be going to Almack's as well?' Geraldine asked him.

'Undoubtedly. Miss Buckley, have you been to Almack's?'

'No, my lord, but I think there was an intention to do so this week.'

'Is that so? In this case I think one of

the first friends I shall call upon are William and Maria Molyneux.'

Geraldine clapped her hands.

'Oh, bravo, Edmund. Lord and Lady Walsh will rue the day they were heartless towards Amanda.' She turned to her new friend to explain. 'Maria, Lady Sefton, is one of the patronesses of Almack's. After Edmund has spoken to her, Lady Walsh will have another screaming fit when she discovers her voucher for Almack's has been withdrawn.

'We must go with him as well when he visits the Seftons, they are a very friendly and entertaining couple. You should ask Lord Sefton about carriage racing. His nickname is Lord Dashalong because of his fondness for racing four-in-hand through the London streets.'

'Geraldine,' Edmund said, reprovingly, 'I don't think his anecdotes are likely to be entirely appropriate for a young lady's ears, especially at a first meeting. I regret you have heard them yourself and I do wish you would erase them from your memory.

'We don't want to give the Seftons the impression Miss Buckley is anything other than entirely correct and proper, in view of rumours the Walshes may be spreading.'

'Ah. No. I had not thought of this. You know, if the Walshes are spreading ugly rumours, should we not be going to London sooner rather than later?'

Edmund rubbed his chin thoughtfully.

'Yes, you are right, we should go no later than Friday. I shall send word today to open Twyford House.'

'Also, Edmund, since we are to be together for some time yet, I do think you should be calling her Amanda, not Miss Buckley all the time. You're not usually so starchy.'

Amanda looked a little uneasy.

'I think this is for Miss Buckley to say, not you, Geraldine.'

'My lord,' Amanda glanced at Geraldine, 'I have no objection. However, only in private if you please, as otherwise, as you say, people may get the wrong idea.'

He thought she had a good point.

If there were stories circulating about her, who was to know how they might become embroidered.

'Thank you, Amanda, do please call me Edmund in return, since 'my lord' will soon become tiresome as well, at least when we are not in the public eye. As for today, I thought Geraldine might like to show you around the house and gardens.'

'But Edmund, I thought you would like to do that,' Geraldine said.

It was clear to Edmund, and perhaps to Amanda as well, that his sister was definitely matchmaking. He would have to have a word with her later.

'No, I'm afraid I have business I must see to this morning, especially if we are shortly to move to Brook Street. In the meantime, Amanda, do you ride?'

'Yes, I do, but it must be months and months since the last time, because of selling up in Calcutta and then the sea voyage. I had a beautiful mare which I gave to my Bengali cousins. I do hope they are looking after her well. I must write and ask them before much longer.'

'In that case, Geraldine, include the stables in your tour and see if the head groom can suggest a suitable mount for Amanda.'

'But Edmund,' Geraldine said, 'if we are to go up to London so suddenly, will we have time to ride before we go?'

'I shall have to go around the estate later today and you could both join me, if you wish. Apart from today, we shall then have to make a little time before we go. If the horse suits Amanda, we shall have all our riding horses taken up to London. We can ride together in Hyde Park.'

'Amanda, do you have a riding habit?' Geraldine asked.

Amanda reflected how events were taking yet another unexpected turn. Only a matter of days ago, she had been living with her uncle and had been escorted in Hyde Park by a handsome young man. Both had turned out to be false friends.

Now she was a guest in the house of an earl and being befriended by his sister.

They seemed genuine and she hoped this proved to be the case.

At least his lordship had no apparent need for money and neither of them seemed to mind about her foreign looks. She had a strong suspicion Edmund not only didn't mind, but actually admired them. Then, as far as she could tell, his servants didn't mind, either, and his footmen were now in awe of Ramesh.

It was all a great relief, but she would have to carefully consider her future. She couldn't remain their guest for ever. She would have to work out what to do next, and before she outstayed her welcome.

'Yes, I do, although I shall probably have to get a warmer one before autumn arrives.

'But first, if you will both excuse me for a short while, I must send a letter to my bank to inform them of my impending move to Brook Street. I think perhaps I should tell my great-aunt Janet, my guardian in Edinburgh, of the recent events as well.'

Amanda worried what her great-aunt

might think. Would she cast her off, too? Could she do so? Even if she couldn't legally disown Amanda, she could still refuse to acknowledge her.

However, it was only right and proper that she be given the full picture. If the worst came to the worst, Amanda could always strike out and set up her own household somewhere. She could certainly afford to do so.

She had heard York was a picturesque city and it might be far enough from London for ugly rumours to not follow her. It would be disappointing to leave her new friends behind, but Geraldine could always visit her in York.

Amanda wondered if there was an Indian or Bengali community somewhere in England where she might be less conspicuous and consequently less prone to unfriendly remarks. It might be easier in such a place to make new friends, too.

Scandal in the Park

'I thought the visit to the Seftons was most satisfactory,' Geraldine said, as they travelled home to Brook Street from Arlington Street.

'Yes, they were very friendly,' Amanda said, 'but she didn't say she would withdraw the Walshes' voucher as you thought she would.'

'No,' Edmund said, as he faced them across the carriage, 'but she did say she would speak to the other patronesses of their and Mellor's behaviour. I think you will find it amounts to the same thing, even if it's not actually Lady Sefton who gives them the bad news. She's much too kind-hearted to do it herself.'

'Shall we ride in the park this afternoon, Edmund?' Geraldine asked.

'I think not, the riding horses will need a rest after travelling all the way from Twyford Hall. However, the carriage horses will be rested and there is the barouche in the carriage house, so

139

you could take it instead.

'Also, I think you two should go on your own, except for footmen, of course, to avoid any whisper of scandal. It will be sufficient for me to be seen with both of you at the Lennons' ball on Monday.'

'Assuming we receive an invitation,' Geraldine said.

'I have no doubt we will. If Maria Sefton sends them a note, thus demonstrating her approval, I'm sure they wouldn't dare not to.'

★ ★ ★

Soon after four o'clock, the earl's barouche pulled by two matched horses rolled into Hyde Park. There were two grooms on the box, two footmen on the back and two young ladies sitting side-byside looking very smug at the picture they knew they were presenting.

Standing behind the blonde, blue-eyed Geraldine in her light blue carriage dress was one of the earl's footmen, complete with white wig and blue coat. Sitting next to her, Amanda, with her nearly black hair and dark eyes, was wearing a dark red carriage dress trimmed with silver embroidery. Behind her was Ramesh wearing a dark red coat with silver braid and a matching cap.

As the barouche rolled slowly through the park, everybody was stopping to watch them go by. Geraldine and Amanda grinned at each other at the impact they were creating, which they were both finding completely gratifying and well worth the afternoon they had just spent discussing how to arrange it.

A horseman trotted over to the side of the carriage.

'Good afternoon, Miss Buckley,' he said, 'I apologise for leaving you at the inn, but you deserved it and should not have lied to me.'

'You!' Amanda said. 'I have nothing to say to you, Mr Mellor, go away.' She turned her face in the opposite direction.

'You said to me you had no money, but a friend at the East India Company says your father was very wealthy and, as his only child, you must be as well.'

'The lady said to go away,' Ramesh said, loudly enough to attract the attention of other people.

'I am a gentleman, you are a servant and a heathen one, too,' Mellor said to Ramesh, getting red in the face. 'How dare you talk to me like that?'

'I dare to say it because you are not a gentleman and I am a Nepali warrior who will be happy to leave scars on your pretty face if you do not leave immediately,' Ramesh said, waving his kukri at Mellor.

Mellor flinched at the angry face of Ramesh, who looked as if he was about to descend from the back of the carriage and carry out his threat. Mellor dug his heels in with a curse and rode away.

'Hah!' Amanda said. 'That told him. I don't think I'll be seeing that particular rat again.' She turned back to Geraldine who was staring at her with wide eyes and a dropped jaw.

'Oh,' Amanda said, realising they had a large audience, 'I wonder if we were wise to create such a stir?'

'I think we will be the sensation of the day, if not of the week,' Geraldine said. 'I know we meant to cut a dash, but perhaps we have overdone it ever so slightly. I fear Edmund is going to be cross with us.'

'Oh, dear,' Amanda said, 'this is not going to make me out to be the image of a proper and respectable lady, is it?'

'No, but I bet all the ladies will now want a fierce Nepali guard.'

* * *

When they reached home, they made a full confession to Edmund. Geraldine was right. He was more than cross. He was frustrated and incensed as he paced up and down in the drawing-room.

'It might not have been so bad if the disagreement had been in a corner of the park with few people to notice. But, no, you go to the park, deliberately attracting attention, and then have a spat in the middle of a crowd with everybody looking on.

'Furthermore, there can be no doubt who you were, with my arms on the side of the coach, the grooms and footman wearing the Twyford livery and Amanda and Ramesh being unique in the whole of London.'

'I'm sorry, Edmund, but it wasn't deliberate, we weren't to know Mellor would be there and nor how he would insult Amanda,' Geraldine said.

'Edmund, I too must apologise for causing you so much trouble. I can see the incident must add fuel to any rumours being spread by my uncle.'

Edmund stopped pacing and took a deep breath.

'No, I know it wasn't the fault of either of you and if it hadn't been for Mellor it would have given an entirely different impression.'

Secretly, he thought the pair of them, sitting side-by-side on the sofa made a quite remarkable picture. He hadn't gone with them to avoid starting any rumours of an improper relationship with Amanda.

Now he regretted not going, as he

would have enjoyed taking Mellor to task instead of Ramesh doing it. Yes, he would have enjoyed being Amanda's defender.

'On Monday evening we have the Lennons' ball. We should go there together and I'm sure the Seftons will lend us countenance as well. I doubt if the Walshes will be present as Maria Sefton probably suggested any invitation be rescinded.

'When we appear at Almack's on Wednesday, and the Walshes don't, I hope any loss in Amanda's reputation will have been restored. You can both make some morning calls on Thursday to see what people are saying by then.'

Geraldine stood and kissed her brother on his cheek.

'Edmund, I am so glad you are my brother. I couldn't wish for a better one to be looking after me.'

He kissed her cheek in return. Edmund felt a bit self-conscious of their display of affection in front of a third party. It didn't seem like a particularly manly thing to be doing.

Edmund's eyes met Amanda's. Her lips twitched as she tried not to smile at them both. He suddenly wished it had been her kissing his cheek, not his little sister. He felt himself starting to blush at the thought, so he gave her a little bow and strode from the room.

Monday arrived, and with it, a letter for Amanda. The butler brought it to her while she was sitting in the morning-room with Geraldine.

'There is a letter for you, Miss Buckley,' he said, offering it to her on a silver salver.

She put down the book she had been reading to take the letter. Was this a reply from Great-aunt Janet? Was it a rejection and a repudiation of the guardianship? Her hands trembled slightly as she opened it. Geraldine sat still and watched Amanda as she read it.

Amanda was very relieved and let out a great sigh. Her great-aunt Janet expressed her disgust at the behaviour of Mellor and the way her uncle had washed his hands of his niece, as well.

Amanda had thought if Janet had disowned her, too, she would have had no family left in the world, save her mother's family back in Bengal. Had this been the case, yes, she could have moved to York or somewhere else, but it would have been hard to start from scratch, not knowing anybody.

As it was, Janet appeared to be friendly and welcoming. She must surely know Amanda's mother had been a Bengali because she corresponded with her father. Of course, once she saw Amanda looked half-Bengali in appearance as well, her attitude could change. After all, her uncle Henry had apparently expected her to look entirely English. However, if she was unconcerned by her appearance and prepared to introduce her to society in Edinburgh, going to live with her guardian might be her best option.

'Is it good news?' Geraldine asked, a little anxiously.

'Yes, she takes my side in the whole affair and seems to share my poor opinion of Uncle Henry. She has also invited me to visit her in Edinburgh.'

'It's encouraging if she wants to see you, although Edinburgh is a long way off.'

'Yes, it is encouraging, at least so far.'

'So far?'

'When she meets me she might be shocked at the way I look. Uncle Henry was horrified and she might be, too.'

'Not everybody is foolish, short-sighted and prejudiced like your uncle. At least a great-aunt is not going to have two daughters to marry off, is she? Were your cousins very ugly? I'm sure I have never met them, or if I have, they were instantly forgettable.'

'No, to be fair, they're not ugly, perhaps just a little on the plain side and rather ordinary. Somewhat dowdy, perhaps, and not very clever, either.

'Letitia is thoughtless and consequently says unkind things sometimes. Her younger sister Felicity is entirely self-interested and tends to speak without thinking, too.'

'Well, there you are; you were a

148

colourful kingfisher with dull brown chickens for cousins.'

Amanda smiled at the analogy.

'I wonder if I should go to Edinburgh to meet her?'

Amanda knew she had to make plans for her future and it would be a way to explore and consider the possibility of living with or near her great aunt.

She would be sad to leave her new friends, but she couldn't become a permanent guest.

'I shall have to give it some thought. This afternoon we shall also have to consider what we shall wear to the ball. It might be wise if we tried not to remind people of how we looked in the park.'

Major Decision

Amanda, Geraldine and Edmund had entered the ballroom and were looking around. Amanda had the impression some of the glances cast their way were a little speculative.

She spotted Freddy Seaton across the room and waved to him.

'Geraldine, do you know Freddy Seaton?'

'No, I don't think so.'

'Well, this is him coming towards us. Now Freddy is lacking in confidence and horribly shy, but perfectly nice and a real gentleman. Once he gets over his embarrassment and relaxes a bit, he also becomes an excellent dancer.'

'Miss Buckley, g . . . good evening,' Freddy said, his ears turning bright red.

'Good evening, Mr Seaton, how lovely to see you again. May I present my friend, Lady Geraldine Nisbet. Geraldine, may I present Mr Seaton.

'He was good enough to lead me out

for my first dance after my arrival in London. I was immensely grateful to him, as otherwise I could have been a wallflower at my first ball, which would have been absolutely dreadful.'

Freddy's cheeks were now growing very pink.

'I . . . I wonder, Miss Buckley, a . . . are you free for the next dance?'

'I regret I am not, Mr Seaton, I have already promised the next one to Geraldine's brother. However, I am free for the following one and I don't think Lady Geraldine is engaged for this one.'

Freddy was shy, but not lacking in understanding.

'Lady Geraldine, may I have the honour of the next dance?'

'I shall be delighted, Mr Seaton.' As she walked away with a hand on his arm, Amanda heard her say: 'It is wonderful to meet a young man who understands how ladies have a horror of being a wallflower.'

'What is amusing you?' a voice asked at her elbow. She turned to see Edmund had joined her and was offering her his hand.

'We are bolstering the confidence of a very worthy young man,' she replied as they joined the set which was forming.

At the end of the set they moved to the side and waited for Geraldine and Freddy to join them.

'Oh,' Amanda said, 'there is Mr Mellor. I had not thought to see him here.'

'Mellor? How very convenient, I wanted a word with him. Which one is he?'

'He is the pretty boy with curly blond hair standing next to the lady in sage green.'

'Excuse me a moment, wait here and I shall return shortly.' He headed around the ballroom to Mellor.

'Mr Mellor?'

'Yes, and you are?'

'The Earl of Twyford. Would you step out to the terrace with me? I need to speak to you for a moment.' He waved his hand towards an open French window.

Mellor looked at him a little suspiciously, but preceded Edmund out on to the terrace.

Edmund realised Mellor hadn't recognised Edmund's crest on the barouche in the park and made the connection. Had he done so, he might not have been so willing to step outside.

They moved a couple of paces away from the French window.

'What did you wish to speak to me about, my lord?'

'I wish to speak to you about Miss Buckley and the abominable way you have treated her.'

'I don't know why either of us should be concerned by an native Indian woman who simply doesn't belong in a society such as ours.'

Edmund punched him hard, full in the face. Mellor, caught by surprise, spun around and fell on to the stone steps leading down into the garden. Edmund watched with satisfaction as Mellor bumped down the steps towards the lawn, then dusted his hands and nodded to himself before turning to re-enter the ballroom. He called a footman over.

'Mr Mellor has fallen down the steps from the terrace and requires your assistance.' The footman looked in alarm towards the terrace before hurrying outside.

Edmund calmly walked back to Amanda, where Freddy and Geraldine also awaited him.

'My lord,' Amanda said, 'what did you do?'

'I explained to Mr Mellor that his behaviour towards you was not acceptable.'

'Was this all?' Amanda asked. It seemed rather feeble to her. Then she noticed Edmund flexing his hand.

'Look!' Geraldine said, drawing their attention to Mellor who was being helped through the ballroom by two footmen. He was holding a bloodstained cloth to his face.

'Hah!' Freddy said. 'Looks like he got a well-deserved lesson from someone. He was always a bully at school.'

Amanda looked at Freddy with wide

eyes, and then her gaze dropped again to Edmund's hand.

'Geraldine,' she said, 'while I am dancing with Mr Seaton, why don't you find a champagne bucket containing ice to sooth your brother's hand?'

Geraldine's eyes also dropped to his hand.

'Oh, well done, Edmund. As I always say, you are the very best of brothers. Come with me,' she said, taking his arm and leading him away.

'Shall we dance, Mr Seaton?' Amanda said, with a twinkle in her eye.

'What happened there? Did I miss something?' Freddy asked.

'What you missed was the Earl of Twyford, Lady Geraldine's brother, teaching Mr Mellor how some behaviours are not tolerated.'

'Did he insult Lady Geraldine? If he did, I shall happily provide him with another lesson.'

'No, Mr Seaton, I was the one insulted, not Lady Geraldine. However, I do appreciate your offer, and you are much more of a gentleman than he is, but I don't think another lesson will be necessary.'

Freddy went decidedly pink around the ears at the compliment as they went to join the set which was forming.

On their way home in the carriage, Edmund looked pensive.

'I've made it worse, haven't I?'

'Not necessarily,' Geraldine said. 'Lady Sefton had been expressing her opinion of both the Walshes and Mellor, too. I dare say many people in addition to Mr Seaton thought he had received his just deserts. No doubt you have risen in many people's estimation by doing something about him.'

'I wonder if he will issue a challenge now,' Edmund mused.

'I shouldn't think he will dare,' Geraldine said, 'he would be terrified of discovering your second was a Gurkha warrior wanting an excuse to cut him to pieces.'

'I could hardly have a manservant as my second, could I?'

'No,' Geraldine said, 'but I bet he keeps well clear of all of us now anyway. I expect he will want to retreat to his parents' house so his injuries have time to heal. I think a pretty face was all he had in his favour.'

'Freddy Seaton was scathing about him. He has made a lot of enemies and not just when he was at school,' Amanda said.

'Apparently he is always trying to borrow money from people and then conveniently forgets the loan. We thought he was a fortune hunter and this just confirms his pockets are always to let.'

'Anyway,' Geraldine said, 'we're both proud of you.' She smiled at her brother.

Amanda was glad to have a champion, but concerned at the trouble she was causing him again. It could so easily all go wrong and damage both his reputation and Geraldine's too. Would people assume Amanda was his mistress and his sister was colluding in the arrangement?

If an idea like this got around, both Amanda's and Geraldine's chances of making a good marriage were nil. There was nothing for it. Amanda would have to give serious consideration to a visit to Great-aunt Janet, at least until all the fuss died down.

* * *

Amanda slept badly, despite being very tired when they reached home. The question of what she should do, was going around and around in her head. Finally, she decided she should go and visit her great-aunt in Edinburgh. Furthermore, she should go straightaway, as any negative talk in London would soon dissipate if she wasn't there to remind people.

First, she had to tell Edmund and Geraldine, then she needed to write to her great-aunt accepting her invitation and to warn her she would arrive in a few days' time. Then she would need to send Ramesh to the bank and to arrange a post chaise on his way back. She went down for a late breakfast and found Geraldine was still there, also having risen late.

'Geraldine, I have decided to visit my great-aunt Janet in Edinburgh. I feel obliged as she is my guardian and at the same time it will give all the talk in London a chance to settle down.'

Geraldine's eyebrows drew together in disappointment.

'I suppose you should go if you must, but I had hoped we could go around together in London for a while, now we are here. We haven't even been to the silk warehouses yet.'

'I know, I know, but I hadn't expected us to create a big commotion. The incident in the park and whatever the Walshes have been saying is bad enough. I dread to think what people might be saying after Edmund sent Mellor from the ballroom with a bloody nose.'

'I'm sure they are saying he got what he deserved.'

'Yes, yes, but if the Walshes say my reputation is ruined and then Edmund, who is no blood relation of mine, strikes Mellor?'

'You mean . . . Oh, surely not?

'I'm sure there are plenty of people out there who have nothing better to do than invent stories and the more the stories are scandalous, the better.'

'If you are going around with me, they will see your reputation is just as good as mine.'

'Or they will say yours is as bad as mine. No, I can't take the risk of ruining both of your reputations. It's best if I go to Edinburgh for a while. I shall be out of their sight and thus out of their minds.'

'For how long will you be gone?'

'I don't know. It will take me three or four days to get there, so I should plan on staying for a while for the long journey time to make any sense.'

Amanda was deliberately vague. She honestly didn't know how long she might be there. It might be for ever, or it could be only a day, or anything in between. If her great-aunt rejected her like her uncle, she might need to make a new home for herself in York or somewhere else. There might even be merit in spending a day or two in York on the way to Edinburgh to see if the city suited her.

'When do you plan to go?'

'Tomorrow. The sooner the better, I think.'

'Are you not going to attend Almack's with me tomorrow night?'

'No. You can go there with Edmund as your escort, it will be perfectly normal and nobody will think anything of it.'

'If you don't go, people will think you have been refused a voucher.'

'Lady Sefton can tell anyone who cares that I do have a voucher and so can you two. You and Edmund can simply explain I have gone to visit my guardian.

'If Freddy Seaton is there, you can tell him to mention, very casually, to his friends where I have gone. He won't mind doing it for us and the word will soon spread.'

Geraldine shook her head sadly.

'I have been enjoying your company and I'm sure Edmund has, too. I shall be counting the days until you return.'

'I promise I shall write to you about all the wonders of Edinburgh.'

'How will you travel? Will you take our travelling carriage? I'm sure we can manage quite well without it for a week or two.'

Amanda knew this was out of the question, especially if she never came back.

'No, it would be a great inconvenience for you. I shall travel post. Ramesh will make the arrangements today.'

'Post? All the way to Scotland? It will be very expensive, how can you manage?'

Amanda realised she had carelessly let the cat out of the bag. She was sure she could trust Geraldine and Edmund, so it was time she told them the truth.

'There is something I have to tell you, and Edmund, in confidence. Some people, like Mellor, have supposed my father was wealthy and therefore I must be wealthy, too.

'I've never actually denied it nor admitted it, I've just told them it was purely supposition, which it was. Those people have then assumed I am not wealthy, when, to tell the truth, I am.'

She could see Geraldine was confused.

'The thing is, when my father was dying he told me to conceal my wealth, otherwise I would be pursued by fortune hunters. He was obviously thinking of people like Mellor.

'The reality was my father worked his way up to a senior position in the East India Company and also married my mother. My mother was one of two daughters. Her father was a wealthy Bengali merchant but had no sons, so my mother brought a lot of money with her to the marriage.

'Mellor said, in the park, a friend of his in the East India Company had told him my father really was wealthy, which of course was true. He said I had lied to him, which was not true, because I just never said so, one way or the other. However, at the time, nobody was really listening to what he said, so nobody has remarked upon it since.'

'And when your uncle threw you out because he thought you were a poor half

Bengali girl of no consequence, he was also making false assumptions?'

'Yes, I'm afraid so. I hope you don't think I've been deceiving you as well. I didn't hire a carriage at the Rose and Crown because I only had a little cash with me, not thinking I would need more than a handful of coins. Besides, I don't think the inn had a vehicle for hire anyway.

'My only deception was one of omission, because I had hoped it wouldn't matter to people if I was rich or poor, and somehow the topic has never arisen until now.'

Amanda felt near to tears. It was bad enough leaving her friends, but to have them think she was deceitful was even worse.

Geraldine came and sat next to her and put her arm round Amanda's shoulders.

'I've hardly ever thought about whether you had money or not. Besides, Edmund has enough money for both of us, all three of us, and so it really didn't matter. We both love you regardless of who you are.'

'And you don't mind how my skin is dark?' Amanda said with a sniffle.

'No, we don't care. Do you mind my hair being blonde?'

Amanda looked at her incredulously, then realised she was joking.

'Silly!' she said and batted Geraldine on the knee.

'Silly? Who's being silly?' an amused male voice asked. As he entered the room, Edmund came to a sudden halt at the sight of the two girls with arms around each other and tears on their cheeks. 'What's wrong? What has happened?'

'Edmund, come and sit down,' Geraldine said, 'Amanda has been confessing sins of omission, none of which matter to me. I doubt they matter to you either. More to the point, she is determined to go to Edinburgh tomorrow.'

Edmund listened carefully while the whole story was repeated for his benefit.

'It seems to me, Amanda, your father gave you good advice. Firstly, flaunting your wealth would have attracted entirely the wrong sort of attention, such as fortune hunters like Mellor.

'Then, secondly, sending Ramesh to give you protection was very sensible too. From what you have said, your father probably guessed his brother wouldn't trouble to take good care of you.

'Personally, I never wondered how much money you had beyond paying the bill at the inn. I supposed you had some sort of income, as you never seemed to be in need or worrying about money.

'No, the only thing you appeared to be in need of were friends and a home, which Geraldine and I have been entirely happy to provide in return for your company. Be in no doubt, you are completely welcome to stay in our house for as long as you wish.'

'Thank you, Edmund. I do appreciate the friendship of both of you, but I am also aware of the trouble I am causing you,' Amanda said. 'Therefore, I am determined to do my duty and visit my great-aunt. It will allow the commotion to settle down.'

'At least take my travelling carriage.'

Amanda shook her head.

'Thank you, Edmund, but no. I cannot tell how long I will be gone and you will surely need it yourself at some point. No, it is out of the question. I shall travel post.'

Edmund felt a pang of fear when she said she didn't know how long she would be gone. He had quickly got used to her being around. He hadn't actually thought about when or if she might leave. Stupid, he knew, but he liked seeing her and talking to her, both at breakfast and dinner.

'We shall miss you,' he said, 'you must write to us as soon as you get there, so we know you have arrived safely.'

Time to Move On

The next morning, Wednesday, the post chaise and four arrived promptly at nine o'clock. Amanda had not wanted to leave any later in case there were delays on the road. She aimed to spend the first night in Stamford and hoped to have time to look around the town before it got dark. She had heard it was an elegant place.

The footmen were loading bags on to the platform at the front of the chaise and the roof, while they said their good-byes at the front door.

Geraldine hugged Amanda.

'Safe journey,' she said, 'be sure to write and tell me everything.'

Amanda nodded and turned to Edmund. He took her gloved hands and raised them to his lips.

'We really shall miss you,' he said. 'Give our regards to your great-aunt, won't you?'

She nodded again, not really trusting herself to speak.

'Goodbye, Edmund,' she whispered and turned to hurry down the steps to where Ramesh was holding the door of the chaise open. She climbed in to join Debjani, Ramesh closed the door, climbed up to the seat at the back and the post boys set everything into motion.

They got only as far as Hanover Square before Amanda lost control of her emotions and burst into tears. Debjani passed her a handkerchief and pulled Amanda into her shoulder.

They had changed horses twice before Amanda was fully back in control. She hoped the ostlers merely thought she was on her way to a funeral or something. It did feel like the funeral of her hopes, because now she recognised she had fallen in love with Edmund and was clear he had felt merely friendship for her. A friendship she would have to put aside, as otherwise she would never be able to move on with her life.

★ ★ ★

They reached Stamford in good time while there was still plenty of daylight left. Amanda went for a short walk around the town with Debjani, while Ramesh dealt with the inn, their bags and the poste chaise.

Stamford, she thought, was a pretty enough town, just as she had been told, but she really wasn't in the mood for sightseeing. She had little appetite, either, and, after a rather perfunctory meal, had an early night.

A good night's sleep meant Amanda's spirits were much revived by morning and she found she could take an interest in the scenery on her way to their next objective, which was Doncaster. She thought this town looked prosperous, but wasn't in the mood to find any enthusiasm for it. It had been another long day cooped up in the carriage with too much time to think. Thoughts about Edmund, which simply wouldn't go away.

Fortunately, the next day it was a relatively short distance to York, giving her less time to sit and think. As soon as they got there, it was immediately apparent there was a great deal to see in the city.

It was still fairly early when they arrived and she was more than ready to stretch her legs with a walk. The inn was right beside a gate in the city walls and it was not far down the street to York Minster, then beyond it to the shops.

'Debjani,' Amanda said, as they walked slowly back to the inn, 'we shall stay here tomorrow and the day after as well. I want to explore the city walls, and some of the shops, too.

'Then, on Sunday, we shall visit the Minster, both to see it and for the church service as well. Perhaps we might stroll along the river later on.'

'It will be a relief not to spend yet another day sitting in the carriage,' Debjani said, 'especially if we have another three days ahead of us to reach Edinburgh.'

'My sentiments exactly. We're halfway to Edinburgh and I'm ready for a break before we continue.' Amanda also saw it was a chance to look around and see if York might be somewhere they could live. So far it looked promising. She could write a letter to Geraldine in the morning, as well.

Thoughts of Geraldine led to thoughts again of Edmund. Amanda banished them from her mind; they could only lead to sadness, regrets and ideas of what her life might have been like at his side, had he returned her feelings.

If only she had not caused him so much embarrassment and notoriety. Even if she hadn't, he might have been ostracised by many people if he had a half-Indian wife. There were British people even in Calcutta who didn't want to socialise with her parents because of her mother. Oh, well, she had left another dream behind her and now must look to see what lay ahead.

Amanda sighed, wondering when it would ever seem as if she was in her own home again. Thank goodness she had the familiar company of Ramesh and Debjani so she didn't feel totally alone.

Over the next two days they explored

the city and Amanda became convinced it was somewhere she could make her home. She didn't know how hard it might be to make new friends in York, although perhaps contact with the churchmen at the Minster might help. Then, while she was looking for a house, she would have to make discreet enquiries about the neighbours, too.

A street where tradespeople lived would be one in which it might be easier to make friends, rather than one where the gentry or the aristocracy lived. She didn't think tradespeople would be as fussy about her origins, especially once they knew her family in Calcutta had been in trade.

As they were walking around the city, Amanda had noticed the Merchant Taylors' Hall. She thought, when she returned to York, it might be a good place to make some enquiries, especially if there was any trading connection between York and Calcutta.

Amanda felt it was a bit depressing, having to make another fresh start, but if it was necessary, then it was necessary. In her letter to Geraldine she tried to hint a little at the idea without actually saying it was her plan.

After all, she might like Edinburgh even better and there she had a family member in Great-aunt Janet. In either case, she liked Geraldine and she didn't want her friend to feel she was being rejected.

Amanda would have to present the idea to Geraldine of living away from London little by little. It also remained for her to see if her great-aunt would be truly welcoming or would reject her, too. In the latter case, she now knew she could come back to York.

Amanda wondered what Edinburgh society would say about someone who had obviously Indian features? Her great-aunt knew Amanda's mother was a Bengali, but knowing it and seeing the result were two different things. Uncle Henry had been rather clearly been taken aback when confronted with his niece who had obviously Indian features.

* * *

By Monday morning they were all refreshed, and set off for Durham as their next overnight stop. The cathedral and castle perched on a bend in the river was a picturesque surprise, so Amanda took the opportunity to look around the city on the following morning.

This meant their departure was rather late and they had only got as far as Alnwick before she called a halt for the day. It was another picturesque town with an imposing castle, but Amanda resisted the temptation to tarry. It would seem like cowardly prevarication and she really had to get to Edinburgh to discover if her destiny was there.

Another early start and with reasonable roads could mean they would arrive in George Square the very next day. Hopefully they would then be done with travelling for a short while. If not, and the visit turned out to be merely duty, she would simply do more sightseeing on her way back to York.

Then, on the return journey, she could visit Alnwick for as long as she wanted.

★ ★ ★

Arriving in Edinburgh, they had no problem finding George Square which they found to be well known. They also had no difficulty being directed to Mrs Johnstone's. This turned out to be a very genteel terraced house on four floors, built of the local stone. Ramesh jumped down and ran up the three steps to rap the door knocker before helping Amanda and Debjani down. They went up to the door as it was being opened by a maid.

'Miss Amanda Buckley to see Mrs Johnstone,' Amanda said.

The maid smiled and bobbed a curtsey.

'Please come in, Miss Buckley, the mistress has been expecting you.'

Almost at once, a slightly stooped white-haired lady emerged from a door into the hall, helping herself along with a walking stick.

'Amanda, my dear, how wonderful to see you at long last. Come into the parlour for tea and tell me everything.' She waved Amanda towards the room from which she had just emerged.

'Your man can send your post chaise away, you won't be needing it. Then Jennie can show your people where to put everything.'

Amanda was relieved. The appearance of herself, Ramesh and Debjani didn't seem to bother her great-aunt in the slightest. In fact, she didn't look the least bit surprised. Did they look as she had expected? Or did she simply not care? Either way, it put one of Amanda's greatest fears to rest immediately.

'Have you eaten this evening?' Mrs Johnstone asked, once they had sat around a table.

'Yes, thank you, a couple of hours ago, when we changed horses.'

'Very good. Now we can all relax. I wasn't too sure when you would arrive, but I guessed you might want to do a little sightseeing along the way.'

Amanda wasn't ready to confide in her great-aunt of any ideas of finding a new place for her to set up home. There was plenty of time to see how she and this tiny fragment of her family got along and, as well, how much she liked Edinburgh.

'Yes, exactly, there is so much for me to see in both England and Scotland. It's all new for me. I thought it sensible to stop a little along the way while I had the opportunity and, besides, it helped to break up a long journey.'

'Quite so. I used to travel down to London sometimes with my husband when he had people to see there and it's a dreadfully long journey.'

'Did you grow up in Edinburgh?'

'Oh, no, I grew up in London. I met my John while he was in London on business. My brother, your grandfather, disapproved of me marrying not just a Scot, but a man who was in trade, too. However, I was of age and determined, so there was nothing he could do to stop us. I have been quite content to live here in Edinburgh.

'After my nephew, your uncle Henry, the current Baron Walsh, made insulting remarks about the Scots on one occasion, I never felt the need or desire to go to London again. I cut the connection and only corresponded with his brother, your father.

'Your father was blamed for something your uncle did and it was the reason your grandfather cast him off. Your uncle wouldn't admit any responsibility or involvement. He is a despicable man and I'll have nothing to do with him.

'John spoke to some Dundee friends in the jute trade and found your father a position in their Calcutta office. He did well there and some years later was persuaded to move to a senior post in the East India Company.'

'I always wondered why he moved to Calcutta, but he never explained it properly.'

'I don't suppose he wanted to talk of it. I expect he wanted to put it all behind him and before long, he wrote to say he had married your mother. After he had married a local girl, he had another reason to not come back, didn't he? He said to me she was very beautiful and I can see you have inherited her looks.'

Amanda blushed at the compliment.

'She was, and they were clearly very much in love. He took it very hard when she died. In a way he didn't seem too distressed when he caught the same fever a few weeks later and expected to die, too. He seemed more concerned about what would happen to me.'

'I was surprised he sent you to your uncle. Maybe he thought his brother might still feel some guilt about what happened before and be ready to introduce you to society in London. Perhaps your father hoped his brother would see it as a way of making amends.'

'I think my uncle's only interest was in expecting I would be bringing him heavy bags of money. I let him assume there was little money to be had, so he soon found an excuse to throw me out.'

'I don't suppose he was happy to find

you have some resemblance to your mother.'

'No, I fear I was a great disappointment to him in many ways.'

'Did he find your manservant alarming, too? He's a fine figure of a man, but not someone I would dare to cross.'

Amanda chuckled.

'Ramesh is a Nepali warrior from the Himalayas and perfectly capable of putting the fear of God into people, no matter which god they happen to follow. He once terrified a fortune hunter who was bothering me in Hyde Park. He swore an oath to my father to protect me and it is very reassuring to have him around. When he went to collect my belongings from my uncle's house, nobody dared stop him.'

'Just as well — your uncle is a mean, nasty, grasping sort of man and you are well rid of him. You are very welcome here. Tomorrow, if you are rested, I shall take you to meet some of your cousins.'

Amanda sat back in amazement.

'Cousins? I didn't know I had any

cousins in Scotland.'

'Well, strictly speaking, they are not really your cousins. They are my great-nephew and great-niece and no blood relation of yours. I suppose that's why they were never mentioned by your father. We never had children, but my brother-in-law had two boys.

'Thomas lives with his family in Arbroath, but Francis lives just in the next street with Moira and they have two children, David and Janet. Anyway, they're my family and you're my family, too, so it's all good enough for me.

'We'll see what we shall do in the morning, but now I'm for bed. I don't stay up late at my age. If there's anything you need, just ask Jennie, but I sure she'll have your servants settled by now.'

'Goodnight, and thank you for your welcome,' Amanda said. Janet just nodded and smiled before making her way to the stairs.

Moments after she left, Debjani came in to join Amanda.

'This house looks comfortable, misa

Amanda. How have you found your great-aunt?'

'Wonderful, she is everything I could have hoped for. She does like to talk, but I'm hoping it means she can tell me many things about my father and grand-parents I didn't know before. She has more nieces and nephews living only a street away whom I will meet tomorrow. I think I shall have an early night, too.'

'Let me take you up to your room which looks extremely comfortable and has a view of the square.'

* * *

The next morning, Amanda was being introduced to the joys of a Scottish breakfast.

'I do like this porridge,' Amanda said, 'it reminds me of some dishes we used to have at home in Calcutta called shujir payesh or shujir halwa. What is it made from?'

'It's made from oats,' her great-aunt said. 'You need something to keep you going all day, especially in winter, and this is a good start. Was the dish which you mentioned made from oats as well?'

'Oh, no, shuji is semolina and our cook used to make it a little sweeter than this, but they are similar sorts of dishes.'

'Well, some people add a little honey to it, but for my taste it has more flavour with a pinch of salt. Now, I sent a message around to Francis inviting him to call with the family later on. By the time we have finished breakfast, the boy should be back with a reply.'

The boy was back before they finished breakfast to say the family would be calling within the hour. Mere moments after they had moved to the parlour from the dining room, Amanda heard the door knocker. The door opened and four people came in unannounced. Amanda rose to greet them.

'Good morning, Aunt Janet,' a big man in a tweed jacket and dark green kilt boomed. 'And you must be Miss Buckley,' he said with a slight bow.

'I'm Francis Johnstone, this is my

wife Moira, son David and daughter Janet, and we're all very pleased to meet you.' The ladies curtseyed and Amanda replied in kind.

'Come along in and sit yourselves down,' Mrs Johnstone said.

As they did so, Amanda looked at them with interest. Francis was tall and solidly built and his son was an only slightly slimmer and younger version of him. He was a handsome young man and probably about the same age as Amanda. His sister was a little younger and well featured, too. The ladies were both tall with very dark hair and were currently removing cloaks, both of which matched the men's kilts.

'Great-aunt Janet says we should consider ourselves cousins, as we are all her nephews and nieces, even if strictly speaking we're not cousins at all. Thus I think you should call me Cousin Amanda, not Miss Buckley, if it is all the same to you.'

'We'll be happy to do so, Cousin, and welcome to your new family,' Francis said with a friendly grin.

'And while we are on the topic, Amanda,' Mrs Johnstone said, 'I would much prefer it if you simply called me Aunt Janet. 'Great-aunt' is such an ageing term.'

'I shall be delighted, and I must say I am very happy to meet everyone,' Amanda said, 'I wasn't quite sure what to expect when I got here and you've all been very welcoming. Now, I see you have matching outfits,' Amanda said, waving a hand at all four of them.

'I told them,' Moira said, 'we couldn't come to meet you without looking like a family, but we don't always dress alike. This is the Johnstone tartan of which we're very proud, I'm not really sure how old it is, but it's what comes from our weaver in Lockerbie. Mind you, until about forty years ago, it was forbidden and we weren't allowed to wear it.'

'I'm glad it's permitted now; it's very nice,' Amanda said. 'Is that a dark blue I can see beside the green under the yellow stripe?'

'Yes, there are some variations on the

theme, but all basically the same sett and same colours.'

'Were you surprised to see men wearing kilts in Scotland?' David asked.

'Well, yes and no. I had not realised it was the custom here, but at home in Bengal the men wear a similar garment called a lungi. It's more comfortable than trousers when the weather is hot and humid. The lungi is usually made of cotton, but it looks as if the kilt is made from wool.'

'Yes,' Moira said, 'when the weather turns cold, you need warm garments. Hot and humid is not usually a problem in Scotland!'

'I think I might fancy getting a cloak like yours, Moira,' Amanda said, 'especially if I'm going to feel like one of the family.'

'Cousin Amanda,' David said, 'I wonder if you would care to walk with Janet and myself this afternoon? We thought to show you the castle and then the Royal Mile. It's only about fifteen minutes' walk from here. We could call in at the kilt maker to see about a cloak, too.'

'Thank you, I shall be delighted.'

After lunch, they sauntered down the Royal Mile after a tour of the castle, with Ramesh and Debjani a little way behind. Amanda had said to Ramesh it wasn't necessary for him to escort her, but he insisted, on the grounds he didn't know the other people and her father would have expected it.

Debjani said she wanted to see a little of the city, too, and would keep Ramesh company. Not only this, she said, but then she and Ramesh would look like a visiting couple instead of Ramesh looking as if he was stalking an enemy. Amanda gave in.

As they wandered down the street, Amanda thought she, David and Janet could become good friends. The two of them reminded her of Edmund and Geraldine. Did all handsome and charming young men have agreeable sisters?

She wondered what the other two might be doing just at the moment. Perhaps they were discussing their triumphs at Almack's on the previous evening.

She felt a pang of jealousy towards any unknown lady who might have captured Edmund's fancy. Amanda told herself this was unreasonable. She had removed herself from their company so their reputations wouldn't became tainted by association with herself. Consequently, she couldn't then complain if they had moved on with their lives. If Edmund started escorting another lady, then she would try to be happy for him.

Amanda had left to make a new home for herself elsewhere. It was starting to look as if Edinburgh might be a viable alternative to York. After all, she now had friends and family here.

'You are looking very pensive, Amanda,' Janet said.

Amanda didn't want to say what she had really been thinking.

'There is a great deal to take in. Edinburgh is quite different from anywhere else I've been. The buildings all look different and even the people dress differently here. And you say there is a palace at the end of the road?'

'Yes, Holyrood. Mind you, it's falling to bits. We could walk a little in the grounds, but it's not somewhere for us to go in.'

Amanda was soon thinking of Edmund again and wishing he was walking with them, too. She kept telling herself she had to forget him and move on, but it wasn't an easy thing to do.

She glanced at David. He was a good-looking man and must surely be in the eye of many young ladies but Amanda realised she felt no jealousy towards those unknown ladies and it was simply because he wasn't Edmund. Would she have felt differently if she had not met Edmund?

It could have happened if her father had told her to come to Aunt Janet instead of Uncle Henry. It would not have been difficult to arrange, because she knew there were plenty of ships going from Calcutta to Edinburgh and Dundee.

Was there a reason he hadn't suggested it? Well, there was no way to find out now. Her thoughts drifted again to London and wondered once more what Edmund might be doing right now. She had to stop this, she told herself; it was becoming an obsession.

Follow the Heart

What Edmund was actually doing at that precise moment was pacing up and down in the drawing-room of Twyford House. He didn't appear to be giving Almack's the least thought, even though the Seftons had enquired about the absence of Amanda.

'Edmund, for goodness' sake, stop fretting, you are making me exhausted. She only left eight days ago and will be back soon enough, most likely in two or, at most, three weeks.'

Geraldine had strongly suspected her big brother had been falling in love with Amanda. Now his agitation and worry was leaving her in no doubt. She was very pleased with the idea on several counts. It was high time Edmund married and she thought Amanda would suit him perfectly.

On top of this, she liked Amanda a great deal herself and the prospect of having her as a sister-in-law was very welcome. Imagine if Edmund wanted to marry someone whom Geraldine found detestable? It would make her life utterly uncomfortable and awkward.

She would then have had to find herself a husband in a hurry, so she could move out to her own house. However, finding a husband in a hurry could be a recipe for disaster.

On the other hand, Geraldine was entirely amenable to living where Amanda was the mistress of the house and the wife of her brother and it was definitely a welcome prospect.

On top of everything, she would no longer have to be the hostess when they had guests and Amanda could look after Edmund instead of her. Geraldine would be free to concentrate on her own friends and marital prospects.

'Are you sure she will be back, then?'

'Sure? Well, no, I can't be sure exactly when she will be back, but no doubt she will tell us when she writes next time.'

'I'm not at all sure she's intending ever to come back,' Edmund said, shaking his head gloomily.

'Not coming back? What do you mean?'

'In her letter she said York seemed like a pleasant place to live. It sounded to me as if she was planning to do exactly that and was giving us a gentle hint.'

'I think you're reading too much into it.'

'And then, when she said goodbye at our front door, it sounded very final.'

'Really?' Geraldine searched her memory, but she couldn't remember anything which sounded so very final. Was Edmund imagining it? Or had she failed to notice something?

'Yes. It struck me as she drove away it had sounded like goodbye for ever. Suppose her great aunt offers her a home? She might decide to stay there for good instead of coming back south. After all, she probably considers herself just a guest here and also thinks she needs to move on somewhere else before we get tired of her.'

'You don't think she feels unwelcome here?'

'No, not really, but I don't think she wants to feel as if she is living on our charity, either.'

'You mean she wants to make her home away from us and from her uncle, too?' This wasn't what Geraldine was hoping for at all. No, it sounded like a really bad plan to her.

'It could be. If you think about it, and if we discount her going back to Calcutta or the Walshes, her great aunt is the only family with whom she could live. It's got to be a possibility. She could easily remain in Edinburgh. We know she can afford to set up her own household wherever she chooses. Do you know what was in the letter from her great-aunt in Edinburgh?'

'No, I never saw it. Do you really fear she won't return?'

'Yes, I do. I know she left some of her belongings here, but there wouldn't have been space in a post chaise. She could just ask us to send it on to her by a carrier.'

Geraldine sighed. Now she thought

about it, she could see Edmund might have a point. As she considered it some more, she saw Amanda hadn't seemed very excited to go to Edinburgh, but more as if it was a sad duty.

Then, when Geraldine had spoken of things they had planned to do together, such as visiting the Greenwich Observatory or the silk warehouses, Amanda hadn't spoken of postponement, had she?

Geraldine contemplated what had been said, and no, definitely, Amanda had merely changed the subject and spoken of other things, quite as if she was no longer planning to do those visits with her any more.

Geraldine considered the business with the Walshes, and then Mellor, and then how Amanda had said she was bringing disrepute to Twyford House.

Amanda had said to Geraldine she would go away for a while to let the fuss, scandal, whatever, to die down. But she hadn't said how long she would be away, had she? No, her only comment had been she didn't know how long she would be gone, and this didn't exclude for ever. Was this why Amanda hadn't mentioned postponing visits to the places they had had in mind?

The more Geraldine mulled it over, the more it seemed Edmund could be correct. Did Amanda think she would embarrass them by remaining here, so her only choice was to leave and not ever return to Twyford House? In which case, if it was not to turn into a disaster for all of them, there was only one answer.

'Edmund, you have to go after her to make sure she comes back. In fact, to maintain the proprieties on the way home, we both have to go.'

'Go? To Edinburgh?'

'Yes, of course to Edinburgh! Where else? I have always wanted to see Edinburgh, now I shall.'

'I'm not sure it makes sense. What if she just wanted to get away from us and was too polite to say? We could get there and everybody would be embarrassed by our arrival. I should have to say we are merely tourists and then I would look foolish because nobody would believe me.'

Geraldine loved her brother, but he could be exasperating sometimes.

'Oh, Edmund, never mind looking foolish in Edinburgh, you are being foolish now. It appears to me, and probably all the servants too, you are in love with her. Furthermore, you probably never gave her the merest hint of it and now she won't know of any good motive to come back.

'You have to follow and tell her of a good reason to come back, which is that you love her. If she really doesn't want to return, I'm sure she will explain it to you gently, before politely sending us on our way. Now tell me I'm wrong.'

Edmund looked, rather sheepishly, at Geraldine. He then paced up and down once more, frowning as he went.

'I can't,' he said at last with a deep and heartfelt sigh.

'Can't what? Can't go? Can't tell her you love her? Can't tell me I'm wrong or can't think of a reason to not go?'

'I can't say you're wrong. I do have to find out if she was planning to come back or not. And if she wasn't, then, as you say, I have to give her a good reason to come home. We shall leave in the morning. Go and tell your maid to pack your things. Romney!' he called loudly, summoning the butler.

'Sir?' Romney said, holding the door open for a grinning Geraldine to pass him by.

'Send word to the mews we are leaving in the travelling coach for Scotland in the morning. Eight o'clock. I want a coachman and groom, two footmen and four horses as I intend to make good speed.

'No, wait, never mind the footmen, I can manage perfectly well without them. Tell my valet to get himself upstairs right now and then tell cook we will want food baskets to take with us. I don't plan to stop any more than necessary.'

★ ★ ★

The next morning the travelling coach drew up at the front door shortly before eight o'clock. As their baggage was being loaded, Edmund went to the front of the carriage.

'I want to get at least as far as the Angel in Grantham today,' he told the coachman.

'Yes, sir, but it must be over one hundred miles to Grantham; it could be dark before we arrive.'

'This is why you have four horses and is all the more reason for leaving at once,' he said, before handing Geraldine up into the carriage to join his valet and her maid.

'Edmund, this may be a foolish question, but do you have the address in Edinburgh?' Geraldine asked, pausing on the last step.

'It's not a foolish question. It must be a large city and we wouldn't want to be asking from door to door, would we? No, I've franked Amanda's letters and I made a mental note. Her great aunt is a Mrs Janet Johnstone of George Square,

Edinburgh. I don't remember the number, but I'm sure it will be easy to discover it when we arrive.'

★ ★ ★

The weather held fair and the Great North Road was in good repair, so they arrived in Grantham just as the light was starting to fade. Edmund was well satisfied by his estimate of time.

Although the Angel was very busy, being well known and right on the Great North Road, it had plenty of room, as he had anticipated, it being a very large inn, much bigger than the Rose and Crown.

The next day they made another early start, but only made it as far as Wetherby before everybody became tired. On arrival, Edmund said they should all retire promptly, because Newcastle would be their next objective and this would require yet another early start.

'Edmund, do we not go to church today?' Geraldine asked the next morning, as they moved away from Wetherby.

'No, I'm anxious to spend as little time on the road as we can. When we arrive, no doubt you can find a church in Edinburgh with evensong if you feel the need to catch up.'

Geraldine glanced at him with a pleased little smile. She could do perfectly well without stopping for a church service if it would get them to Amanda more quickly.

She knew people would frown upon them for travelling on a Sunday, but just at the moment, she didn't care. Edmund was certainly determined and anxious to find Amanda as soon as he could.

Geraldine picked up her book, glad she had brought several. Never mind finding evensong in Edinburgh, she hoped the city had some good bookshops, so she could prepare for the return journey. They might have something new by Walter Scott and she had nearly finished 'Waverley'. Hopefully he had written another book or two by now.

After an hour or so, Edmund interrupted her reading.

'I'm a little surprised there has been no trace of Amanda and her servants along the way,' he said. 'I would have thought more ostlers and gatekeepers would remember them. Even if they don't notice the ladies inside, they surely notice Ramesh on the back perch. I mean, he is pretty distinctive and there can't be many Gurkhas passing this way. However, nobody seems to have noticed them after we passed Stilton.'

Geraldine put a finger in her book to keep her place.

'Perhaps they took a different road. After Stilton they might have gone to Peterborough to see the cathedral and afterwards on to Lincoln to see that cathedral as well.'

'I suppose they could, but surely they would take the quickest way to Edinburgh? It's long enough as it is. She's not a big enthusiast for old buildings, is she?'

'No, not as far as I am aware. Mind you, when she wrote her letter she was in York and remarked upon the city walls and the Minster. England is completely new to Amanda and she might fancy seeing a little of it before they get to Scotland.

'Considering she went through York and we are at present passing it by, it wouldn't be a surprise if she took a completely different route before as well, would it?'

'I suppose not,' Edmund said, 'especially if she doesn't plan to come back south to England ever again.'

His valet and her maid glanced at each other briefly, but passed no comment.

'Edmund, don't be so gloomy! I'm sure when we get to Edinburgh she will not only be surprised, but happy to see us, too.' At least, Geraldine hoped she would be glad to see them. Amanda would definitely be surprised at their arrival, but would she be pleased at Edmund pursuing her all the way to Scotland — or dismayed he wouldn't leave her alone?

Geraldine desperately hoped she would welcome them, otherwise this was going to be a rather lengthy wild goose chase. Never mind, she had nothing better to do and it really would be interesting to see Edinburgh.

* * *

By the time they got to Newcastle, it was apparent that everybody, coachman, groom, valet, maid, Edmund and Geraldine were all getting sick and tired of the incessant travelling.

It did not help that for the last afternoon the weather had been a persistent drizzle. Edmund decreed the next stage should be even shorter and only to Berwick. They could perhaps have reached Edinburgh in only one more day, but he didn't want to arrive at Mrs Johnstone's door late in the evening, with everyone exhausted and possibly wet, too.

From Berwick to Edinburgh was little more than half a day's travel, meaning they could easily arrive in mid-afternoon.

He had no idea if Mrs Johnstone could house them all, and if not, then they would have to find themselves an inn or hotel. It was another reason for not arriving late in the evening. He didn't suppose finding somewhere to stay would be a difficulty in Edinburgh.

In the event, they arrived in George Square at a sensible time. They had had no difficulty being directed to Mrs Johnstone's house.

The valet helped Edmund and Geraldine down while the groom ran up the three steps and knocked at the door. Edmund and Geraldine went up to the door as it was opened by a maid.

'The Earl of Twyford and Lady Geraldine Nisbet to see Mrs Johnstone,' Edmund said, handing over his card.

The maid looked surprised and her eyes flicked to the carriage, complete with crest on the door. Then she bobbed a nervous curtsey and took the card.

'If you would step inside please, my lord, I will see if Mrs Johnstone is available.' She hurried down the hall into a room at the back, before returning almost at once behind a lady tapping her way down the hall with a walking stick.

'My lord,' she said, 'welcome. My great-niece Amanda has mentioned your name to me. Come you both into the parlour.' She pointed to the door which had been opened by the maid.

Once they were sitting around a tea tray, she turned to Edmund.

'So, my lord, as I said, I know your name from Amanda, but what brings you to Scotland?'

'Ah, um, well, you see . . . Amanda, Miss Buckley, had been talking about coming to Edinburgh,' Edmund said. 'After she left, my sister expressed a wish to visit Edinburgh for herself and urged me to bring her.'

'Oh, is that so?' Mrs Johnstone said, raising an eyebrow and nodding her understanding.

Geraldine suspected Mrs Johnstone was sceptical, and might actually be guessing the truth of the matter. She took pity on her brother.

'It's true. After Amanda left, I told him he was being foolish by letting her go on her own while we stayed at home, when we could have easily come with her. I told him we should go as well. All being well, we could meet up with Amanda here and then all of us see Edinburgh together.' She smiled knowingly at Edmund who was looking uncomfortable and embarrassed. 'Is Amanda not here?' Geraldine asked.

'She has gone shopping with her cousins, David and Janet Johnstone. I expect her back in an hour or so.'

'She has cousins here?' a surprised Geraldine asked. 'She never mentioned any Scottish cousins.'

'Well, let us call them honorary cousins. They are my great-niece and great-nephew, so they are not strictly related to Amanda. It's convenient they are of a similar age and so can go about together. Anyway, enough of this, would you care to stay here with me while you're in Edinburgh?'

'Thank you, Mrs Johnstone, but we have our servants outside, so we should find ourselves an inn or hotel,' Edmund said.

'No, no, you two stay here with me. It will be grand having you three young people staying in the house. You can send your carriage and servants around the corner to an inn called the Apple Tree. Then you can send the kitchen boy to fetch them whenever they're needed.

'No doubt you, my lord, can mostly fend for yourself and Miss Geraldine can borrow my own or Amanda's maid for a while, so I can easily find room enough for you both.

'Now you tell them to bring in your bags and afterwards the boy can show them where to go.'

'If you don't mind, Mrs Johnstone,' Geraldine said, 'I would like to freshen up first and then take a turn around the square with my brother, because we've been cooped up in the carriage far too much in the last few days.'

'Certainly. Jennie will take you upstairs while his lordship speaks to your servants.'

* * *

A short while later, their carriage had trundled away with a pleased kitchen boy sitting on the box between coachman and groom. Edmund and Geraldine were strolling slowly around the square.

'Well, Edmund, I must say Mrs Johnstone is very friendly but I'm not at all sure she believed we're here because I was desperate to see Edinburgh,' Geraldine said, as they sauntered along. 'I'm fairly sure she thought we had a different motive.'

Edmund was quite certain they hadn't been believed, but their hostess was clearly too polite to suggest otherwise. He wondered how long they could stay without becoming a nuisance. If Amanda didn't welcome their arrival, they should remain no more than a couple of days. It would surely be enough to see the principal sights of the city. Then they could excuse themselves and leave on the grounds of visiting other places.

Berwick-upon-Tweed was surely worth

more than their brief stop on the way north, then there was Holy Island, Bamburgh Castle, and oh, so many other worthy places to make their tourism plausible.

It would also give him time to lick his wounds before reappearing in London society. Or it might be better to retreat straight to Twyford Hall for a while, to let any remaining speculation about him and Amanda dissipate.

On the other hand if, wonder of wonders, Amanda welcomed his arrival, he would need to find a way to be alone with her for a while. There were things he needed to say to her in private. He hoped he would find the words to express what he felt and see if his feelings were reciprocated.

Edmund knew talking about feelings wasn't something he was good at. Delivering a speech in the House of Lords was a lot less intimidating.

Of course, even if she was happy to see the two of them, it could be she was merely happy to see her friends, but nothing more.

'Look!' Geraldine said, shaking his arm and thus shaking him from his wool-gathering, 'isn't that Amanda entering the square on the other side?' She waved her arm energetically in a quite unlady-like manner to attract Amanda's attention.

Edmund looked across the square, his heart jumping at the prospect of seeing Amanda again. Then his heart sank. Yes, it was Amanda, but she was clinging to the arm of a young Scotsman and smil-ing adoringly up into his face. It didn't look as if she had missed him at all.

There was a younger girl with them, too, who said something to Amanda while pointing towards Edmund and Geraldine.

Amanda stopped for a moment, looked at them intently and then, dropping the man's arm, hurried towards them, with the other two following slightly more slowly.

'Edmund, Geraldine, what are you doing here?' Amanda said, a little breath-lessly, as she reached them.

It wasn't quite the loving welcome Edmund had hoped for and his heart sank even further. It looked as if he had already lost her to a Scotsman, although he wasn't sure if she had ever been his to begin with. A Scotsman, who, if he had understood Mrs Johnstone correctly, was no blood relation to Amanda and therefore perfectly eligible as a possible husband.

'We, I mean Geraldine, realised after you had left she also wanted to see Edinburgh, so we decided to come to Scotland as well. Mrs Johnstone has just invited us to stay with her for a couple of days.'

From the corner of his eye, he noticed Geraldine frowning up at him. The other two people came to join them.

'I am supposing your friends here are David and Janet Johnstone, whom Mrs Johnstone mentioned. Will you introduce us?' Edmund said.

'Oh, yes, I do beg your pardon,' Amanda said. 'David, Janet, may I introduce Edmund, the Earl of Twyford and his sister, Lady Geraldine.'

Edmund bowed to Janet and shook hands with David as they sized each other up. Geraldine gave him a despairing look and then embraced Amanda like a sister.

'Amanda, you must tell me all the exciting things you have been doing and seeing while you have been here,' Geraldine said, taking Amanda's arm and walking on with her without waiting for the others. 'Perhaps you and your cousins can show us them, too, before we head home.'

Edmund watched them for a moment with a raised eyebrow before turning back to the other two.

'They have become like sisters,' he explained as the three of them followed, 'which is why Geraldine regretted not coming with Amanda. We had a letter from Amanda telling us all about York and Geraldine realised at once what we were missing.' He didn't feel the need to explain it was a whom, rather than a what, which had been missing.

'Did you visit York as well, my lord?'

Janet asked.

'Er, no,' Edmund said, realising he had to continue making up the story, 'but we plan to stop there on the way back home. There are a great many things and places to see along the way, so we shall be taking our time on the way back.'

'Will Amanda be returning with you, do you suppose?' Janet asked.

'To be honest, I have no idea what her plans might be,' Edmund said, realising this was the absolute truth. He had been hoping she would return with him, but after seeing her with David Johnstone, he was filled with doubts.

She had left London hurriedly and before their names could be linked. Had she now formed an attachment to this David, whom Edmund reluctantly recognised was a notably handsome and eligible young man?

Amanda had been surprised to see Edmund and Geraldine in the square. Their coming to Edinburgh had never crossed her mind. In the event, she was suddenly very glad to see them again, especially Edmund, although she was a little dismayed at his cool reception.

At least the warmth of Geraldine's embrace meant one of them had been happy to see Amanda once more. Perhaps it was as he had said, and they were here at Geraldine's urging, not his.

'If you have been travelling, I don't suppose you've received the letter I sent from here,' Amanda said.

'No, we've only received the one you sent from York. What did your latest one say?' Geraldine asked.

'Oh, something about the city and how it was nice to discover I wasn't Great-aunt Janet's only great niece.'

'Nothing about it being a good place to live?'

Amanda looked sharply at Geraldine. Had Geraldine realised Amanda was considering setting up house away from London? What could she say to her friend? As soon as Geraldine spoke again, Amanda saw she had hesitated too long before replying.

'Because your letter from York sounded

as if you might not be coming back to Twyford House.' Geraldine sounded reproachful. 'It's what made me concerned and unhappy you might not want to come home. Edmund was agitated at the idea as well and miserable, too.

'The truth is, we had to come and find out. If you don't want to come back, we can't make you, but we'll both be disappointed. If you want to stay here instead, I'll still be your friend.'

Goodness, a silent Amanda thought, do I have more choices than I had thought?

'But I was an embarrassment to both of you. My reputation was hanging by a thread and if mine is ruined by Mellor and my uncle, yours will be ruined by association. I had to go away to avoid it happening. It won't take long before I am a distant memory and then the whole scandal will soon be forgotten. Both of you will soon be restored to how things were before you ever met me.'

'Have you considered we don't want to be restored to how we were before?

217

Especially not Edmund.'

Amanda stared at Geraldine. What was she suggesting? But they were approaching Mrs Johnstone's house and this discussion would have to be continued another time. She saw the other three were also close behind them now, before she looked back again to Geraldine.

'So are the shops any good here?' Geraldine asked, to change the topic.

'Yes, I must show you without delay,' Amanda said, happy for it to be switched, so she might have time to consider what Geraldine had been saying.

'I have just bought a very fine pair of gloves and tomorrow there will be a new cloak ready for me to collect. I have been persuaded to buy a cloak of the same green and yellow tartan the Johnstone family favour.'

Geraldine could see her two favourite people in the world were both being stupid. Clearly it was up to her to give them a nudge. Geraldine turned to face Janet as they waited for the door to be opened.

'Perhaps you and Amanda could

take me around the shops tomorrow? Amanda says she has a cloak to collect, anyway. No doubt there are any number of fine buildings to be seen as well, but first I want to do a little shopping.'

Both men looked sufficiently alarmed at the idea but a little later, Geraldine managed to get her brother alone for a moment, at which point he was informed he would absolutely insist on escorting them to the shops or she would never speak to him again.

She stared at him hard until he understood it was an order and he didn't have a choice, at which point he nodded agreement.

Sealed With a Kiss

'No, no, I absolutely insist on coming with you,' Edmund said, the next day. 'I have to keep an eye on my sister's spending, and besides, you will need someone to carry all the packages, won't you?'

Edmund wasn't sure exactly what his sister had in mind, but he knew from experience he must to do what she wanted if he was to have any peace. She had said she would endeavour to leave him alone with Amanda at some point.

He also knew he had to find out if he and Amanda had any future and furthermore, he had to find out soon, so it wasn't difficult to agree with his sister.

All the same, he wasn't looking forward to what could be a humiliating conversation. Still, if Amanda preferred to stay with David Johnstone instead of him, he had to clarify it, otherwise he would always wonder. It would be ridiculous to be heading home and still not know.

He had said to Mrs Johnstone they would only be here for a couple of days, so he had to get on with this discussion if it was not to become a rather awkward situation.

'Shall we call at my house and see if David wants to join us?' Janet asked, who had arrived a few minutes before. 'We only live around the corner in Buccleuch Place.'

'No, we don't need to trouble him,' Geraldine said, 'I'm sure you and Amanda are quite sufficient as guides. While we are passing the shops, remember I would also like to call at a good bookshop. I want to see if there is anything new by Walter Scott.'

'There is. His most recent one is called 'The Heart Of Midlothian'. In fact, before we call at a bookshop, let us visit the Heart of Midlothian itself.'

'Oh? What is it?'

'It's a marker on the ground where the prison used to be a few years ago. The prison has been gone a while, but there is a heart-shaped stone mosaic on the street now to mark the spot, right by St Giles Cathedral.'

The group walked down the hill to the high street talking of nothing in particular. Geraldine made a point of taking Janet's arm, which then meant Amanda had to take Edmund's arm.

Edmund had always thought his sister was bit of a schemer and now she was excelling herself. Not that he minded this time, as he was enjoying walking with Amanda. He found it wasn't far to the mosaic in the street, which they duly admired.

'Janet,' Geraldine said, 'Amanda was telling me about the cloak she has ordered and I wonder if the shop over there, across the street, might have something similar which would suit me.'

Janet looked at the shop at which Geraldine was pointing.

'It might,' she said a little dubiously, 'but it's not the one we went to yesterday.'

'Never mind, come, let's take a quick look,' she said, pulling gently on

Janet's arm. 'Edmund, you wait here with Amanda, we shall only be a moment.'

Edmund watched his sister depart before turning to Amanda.

'You know,' he said, 'there are times when I wonder if I really know my sister at all.'

'What do you mean?'

'When you left us to visit your guardian here in Edinburgh, I thought it was just a duty visit and you would soon be home again. Nevertheless, I missed you and was counting the days until your return. Then we got your letter from York and Geraldine said it definitely sounded as if you were thinking of living there.'

'To be honest, Edmund, I have been considering it.'

'But why? Were you so unhappy with us?'

'No, but after the business with my uncle and Mellor, I could only be damaging your reputation and Geraldine's, too, by my presence. To mend things I simply had to go away.'

Edmund's confidence returned. She

had gone away because she cared about them, not because she didn't, or for some other vague reason.

'But that's nonsense and we don't want you to go away. As Geraldine made me realise that day, I'm in love with you and I could see my heart had gone off to Edinburgh with you. I had to come and fetch you home. To our home.

'Trust Geraldine to bring us to this exact spot, The Heart of Midlothian, for me to tell you how you have my heart in your hands. I desperately want you to come home with me and never leave my side again.' He took her hands and held them to his chest.

'I can't; it would ruin Geraldine's marriage prospects,' she said, looking very sad. 'Everyone would say you have taken a poor Bengali girl as your mistress and it would be a huge disgrace for your sister to befriend me.'

'What? No, no, no! You misunderstand me. I want you as my wife. As the next Countess of Twyford and then you will have a reputation nobody will dare impugn.

'Of course, I realise you might want to stay here and prefer marriage to someone else, in which case we will go away tomorrow to avoid embarrassing you any further.'

'Marry someone else? No, it is out of the question, there is nobody else I want to marry, there is only you. I have loved you since the moment you walked into my room at the Rose and Crown.'

Edmund could hardly believe his ears.

'Thank goodness!' he gasped. 'In that case, will you marry me, Amanda?'

'Yes, Edmund, I will, and as soon as we may.'

Edmund released her hands to embrace her and pull her closer. As he bent down to place a tender kiss on her lips, there was a burst of clapping around them. They looked around and saw they had gathered a little crowd of interested onlookers, including Geraldine and Janet.

'Oh, dear,' Edmund said, 'I hadn't meant to ask you in such a public place.

We've become the spectacle of the day.'

'I hope,' Geraldine said, coming a little closer, 'this means Janet and I can become attendants to the bride.'

'I should like it very much,' a beaming Amanda said. 'I suppose this means we all need to be shopping right now for some suitable dresses as well as a cloak and a book.'

'First of all, I think we should find a jeweller,' Edmund said. 'There is a matter of finding my fiancée a suitable betrothal ring. Janet, where do you suggest?'

* * *

On their arrival back in George Square, Edmund and Amanda sought out Mrs Johnstone. Geraldine and Janet followed them in to the parlour.

'Mrs Johnstone, I have asked Amanda to marry me and she has consented, but I am conscious you are her guardian. She is under age and perhaps I should have asked you first.'

226

Great-aunt Janet beamed.

'Don't you be worrying about that! I am very pleased for you both, and you have my blessing. However, you are in Scotland now and don't need my blessing. I have to say, I'm sure my nephew, Amanda's father, may God rest his soul, would have been very pleased, too.'

'In any case, according to Scottish custom, you're already married to each other,' Janet said.

'Already married?' Edmund said. 'How can it be so?'

'Because you stood in the middle of the high street of Edinburgh and, in front of witnesses, declared your willingness to marry,' Janet said, 'and that is all it takes in Scotland.'

Edmund and Amanda stared at each other with wide eyes.

'Hush, Janet,' her great aunt said, 'what you say is true, but it won't do for an English earl. People will call it into question and say it was an irregular marriage. No, they should marry in the kirk, so none can argue with it.'

Edmund was, on the one hand, amazed they might already be married. A little disappointed, too, as he had hoped to savour the moment. On the other hand, he had actually been looking forward to marrying Amanda quickly, as he knew it was possible to marry immediately in Scotland.

Now, paradoxically, he was a little dismayed at a delay, just so they could be married, and married indisputably, in a church.

'Here in Scotland I suppose we will need banns to be read in church, just as in England?' he asked.

'Yes, I'm afraid so, but you won't necessarily have to wait for three weeks.'

'We won't? Why not?'

'I think if you go to my usual church, mention how anxious you are to return to England as a married couple and also the generous donation you will be giving the church, you may find they can read the banns three times in the same Sunday.'

'Really? All three on the same day?'

'Yes, it would not be the first time. Besides, I expect the minister will be gratified you wish to be married in their church.'

Edmund was astonished by the whole business. It seemed in Scotland they made it easy for people to marry, whereas in England they put obstacles in your way.

'In this case, I think my fiancée and I should go and see the minister at once. I should be happy for us to be married next Monday if it can be done,' Edmund said, looking at Amanda, who nodded enthusiastically.

'Geraldine,' Janet said, 'in this case we should go back to the modiste tomorrow and make sure our new dresses are finished by the weekend.'

'Yes, but do you think it might be even better if we go right now?'

'If you do,' Amanda said, 'take Debjani with you for propriety. Oh, speaking of Debjani, and Ramesh, too, Edmund and I need to speak with them before you go. Geraldine, pull the bell please.

Edmund, come into the dining-room so we can speak to them alone.'

Amanda spoke to Edmund as they waited in the dining-room for the servants to appear.

'Edmund, my father is not here to give me away. I could ask Francis Johnstone, but do you mind if I ask Ramesh instead?'

'Not at all. As he has been acting on your father's instructions, it would seem appropriate to me.'

Ramesh and Debjani entered the room and looked expectantly at Edmund and Amanda.

'His lordship has asked me to marry him and I have agreed,' Amanda said. 'We are thinking of getting married next Monday in the local church if the minister is agreeable.'

'Congratulations, I'm sure Misa Amanda's parents would have been very happy,' Debjani said and Ramesh bowed to them.

'Ramesh,' Amanda said, 'I have a favour to ask of you. My father is not here to escort me up the aisle, but you have been protecting and safeguarding me in the same way as my father would have been doing. Would you be kind enough to escort me up the aisle and hand me into the new protection of my husband?'

'I shall be deeply honoured, Misa Amanda and happy to think I have completed my oath to your father,' Ramesh said with a deep bow.

'Ramesh,' Edmund said, 'I have another favour to ask of you. I will be grateful if you will join our household, although you are naturally free to go elsewhere, perhaps back to Calcutta at my expense, if you so choose.'

'My lord, I shall be content to continue in the service of Misa Amanda and yourself. I have no desire to go elsewhere.'

'Excellent. I am planning to buy another curricle here in Edinburgh. After the wedding, my new countess and I will journey on our own, in a leisurely way, back to our home in Twyford Hall. Everybody else will need to return in my travelling carriage.

'I would like you to be in charge of making sure everybody returns safely. In particular, my sister, Lady Geraldine, will be on her own and I would like you to care for her, in the same way as you have been caring for your mistress until now.'

'Your confidence and trust in me is deeply gratifying, my lord.'

'Good, and thank you. Now, Amanda, let us visit the minister, then our servants who are enjoying a rest at The Apple Tree, and finally Francis and Moira Johnstone too.'

On their return, Edmund sought out their hostess to tell her everything was arranged for Monday. Geraldine took Amanda to one side.

'Amanda,' she said, 'something has occurred to me. When you are married you will be the Countess of Twyford and will considerably outrank your uncle and aunt. Nobody will think it strange if you look down your nose and give them the cut in public. It will serve them right for what they did to you.'

'No. You are correct, but I wouldn't want to do it. I've had far too many people look down at me before, and snub me as well, to want to do the same to any other people.

'No, I will be civil if necessary or otherwise just ignore them. I might even invite my cousins Felicity and Letitia to visit us without their parents. Then they can see that not everybody has the same attitude as my aunt and uncle.

'I wonder if they would be allowed to visit Aunt Janet as well? After all, she is their great-aunt, too, and they need to understand the Scots are just as worthy as the English, even if their father doesn't believe it.'

Happy is the Bride

They married in the local church on Monday morning, in the presence of all the servants, their handful of family members and a scattering of interested neighbours. Francis had engaged a piper to lead them in. David was acting as Edmund's best man. Moira had presented Amanda with a small bouquet of flowers containing a sprig of white heather.

'It is traditional and for good luck,' she had explained.

After the ceremony they had then walked around, in a somewhat ragged procession, to the Apple Tree for the wedding breakfast. The piper led the earl with his new countess, followed by David with Geraldine on one arm and his sister Janet on the other. Then Francis had Moira on one arm and his aunt Janet on the other.

The family were few in number and could have squeezed into the house in George Square but they had decided to have it at the inn and be joined by all their servants.

Francis didn't think the Earl of Twyford was particularly high in the instep, but he had felt a little explanation before the wedding was in order.

'It's not,' he had said, 'a question of us being especially egalitarian. It's more a question of having enough people for at least a four couple set. Aunt Janet is unable to dance these days and we simply can't have a wedding without a little dancing.

'We've small households and are inevitably closer to our servants than you would be with a large house and an estate. Therefore, if we are to have an eightsome reel, as everyone will expect, we need more bodies willing to dance.' Francis didn't notice a slight amount of alarm in Edmund's face at the prospect of him performing Scottish dances.

At the end of the meal, when the quaich had been filled and passed around several times, it was time for the dancing, made clear by a fiddler tuning his instrument in readiness.

'Edmund and Amanda,' David said, coming to stand behind them, 'we're going to have a little dancing now, but as I don't suppose you are familiar with Scottish dances, shall I start it off with Janet?'

'Thank you, David, but it's not necessary,' a smiling Amanda said, 'because I'm sure Edmund and I can manage as the first couple to lead the set. If Edmund is unsure of the steps, I can prompt him a little as we go.'

'Do you know any Scottish dances?' David asked Amanda with a puzzled frown.

Amanda chuckled.

'Oh, yes. You forget there was a large Scottish community in Calcutta, a lot of whom came from Dundee because of the jute trade. Provided the piper or the fiddler can play something like 'Petronella' or 'The Duke of Atholl's Reel', we'll be fine.' She noticed her new husband looked a little worried at the prospect.

'Oh, David, wait a moment. I know

'The Haymakers' is often played as the last dance, but let us have that one first, as it is a very sociable dance and will get everyone mixing.'

David nodded and went off to speak with the musicians. Edmund looked relieved.

'I thought I was going to be revealed as the one person in the room who didn't know what he was doing. I'm so glad I married an intelligent woman who knows how to look after me.'

Amanda gave him a broad smile and kissed his hand.

Later on, the room was full of noise, laughter and energetic dancing.

Edmund judged it was time for them to leave, even though the party promised to continue for some while yet. He had already given Ramesh a suitably large packet of money to cover the expense and their return. Edmund hoped to reach Melrose by the end of the afternoon, where he had been assured there were several good inns and a picturesque abbey.

'Amanda, my dear,' her great aunt said, as the newlyweds were moving around the room to say their goodbyes, 'I waited nearly twenty years to meet you, but you must come again soon.

'Another twenty years will not do, for fairly obvious reasons, and you are both welcome to come any time. Edmund, and I will presume to call you Edmund, now you are family, you take good care of her and hasten back as soon as you may. Should you wish to send Geraldine to me for a little holiday, she will be welcome too and especially now she has friends here as well.' She dabbed a tear from her eye.

Finally they moved to Geraldine who embraced Amanda.

'Amanda,' she said, 'I am so happy to have you as the sister I never had before. I am sure you will look after Edmund, so I no longer have to worry about him myself. He is an excellent brother and I am sure he will be an equally excellent husband.'

'Geraldine, I am just as happy to have

you as a sister who has been my friend since the day we met. Ramesh is now your personal manservant and all the other ladies will be jealous of you when you ride in the park. I know he will protect and take care of you on your way back to Twyford Hall, where we will join you in two or thee weeks.'

Everybody moved out to the front of the inn where Edmund's shiny new curricle stood waiting with their bags strapped to the board at the back and his groom holding the horse.

Edmund handed Amanda into the carriage before joining her. He drew some handfuls of silver from his pocket and tossed them to the servants, making sure some fell near the kitchen boy. They drove away from the cheering and waving crowd with Amanda waving goodbye to everybody.

After they had travelled a little way, Amanda moved close to Edmund, took his arm and rested her head on his shoulder.

'I have to say,' she said, 'I never thought

I would fall in love with and marry an English earl in Scotland. In fact, when I left Calcutta, any of this would have seemed like a fantastical dream.'

'For my part,' Edmund said, 'I never thought to fall in love with and marry the mysterious lady at the Rose and Crown. Mr and Mrs Thomas will be completely astonished next time we see them. In fact, we must make a point of calling at the inn on our way home. And one more thing. I owe Geraldine a new hat. I think it should be a particularly nice hat, too.'

'A new hat?'

'Yes, let me explain . . .'

We do hope that you have enjoyed reading this large print book.

Did you know that all of our titles are available for purchase?

We publish a wide range of high quality large print books including:
**Romances, Mysteries, Classics
General Fiction
Non Fiction and Westerns**

Special interest titles available in large print are:
**The Little Oxford Dictionary
Music Book, Song Book
Hymn Book, Service Book**

Also available from us courtesy of Oxford University Press:
**Young Readers' Dictionary
(large print edition)
Young Readers' Thesaurus
(large print edition)**

For further information or a free brochure, please contact us at:
**Ulverscroft Large Print Books Ltd.,
The Green, Bradgate Road, Anstey,
Leicester, LE7 7FU, England.
Tel:** (00 44) **0116 236 4325
Fax:** (00 44) **0116 234 0205**

Other titles in the
Linford Romance Library:

CHRISTMAS ON THE ISLE OF SKYE

Kirsty Ferry

The Isle of Skye is a magical place, especially at Christmas, and there's nowhere Zac Fallon would rather be. But whilst Zac has everything he needs on Skye, there's still something missing — and that something is a somebody called Ivy McFarlane. Ivy used to work with Zac, but then spread her wings and moved to Glastonbury. He's missed her ever since. Now it's almost Christmas, and Zac realises that the Ivy-shaped hole in his life is too big to bear . . .